THE QUAVERING AIR

The Quavering Air

Simone Snaith

High Aldwin: "The power to control the world is in which finger? . . . When I held up my fingers, what was your first impulse?"

Willow: "Oh . . . it was stupid."

High Aldwin: "Just tell me."

Willow: "To pick my own finger."

High Aldwin: "Aha, that was the correct answer."

— *Willow* (1988)

Chapter One

Renna hesitated outside the crowded entrance to the Observatory Hearth, her heart knocking against her chest. Her grip on her staff was slick with sweat. Old Barrin had worked so hard to prepare her, but right now, it seemed like it was all for nothing. Because she could not imagine crossing that threshold and answering the Appon's call.

But the droves of other people jostled her through it and into the glittering hallway. She stumbled along toward the assembly, still unable to fully grasp what she had been assigned.

To join a company of champions—*champions!*—that must travel to the Time Tower and reset the Two Clocks.

The gathering hall gleamed with crimson light from its vaulted stained glass windows. Rich, somber red was the signature color of the Appon. Their robes and the lining of the elegant chairs behind them were of the same hue. Its warmth radiated into Renna and helped calm her nerves.

She recalled the dark red kerchief her mother kept tied in a knot on her hearth back in the village. It was a reminder to consider things wisely and calmly, as the Appon always did.

In the dome above the hall hovered the great Avidian stone from which the wise ones could project their astral forms to look out upon the world. That was how they had seen for themselves that the tall, dark Time Tower now shimmered behind a protective spell-shield.

The lights were so bright in the hall, unlike the simple candlelight of Toom. Back there in her village . . . her six years of Umbra training with the formidable Barrin had allowed her to believe she might be a champion—perhaps. But out here in the world, among the great warriors of countless regions and races . . .

The only true combat she had seen was two years before, when Neyden raiders had attacked her village in the night, on their way to much bigger spoils. The first time the lupine marauders had descended, they'd killed many, including Renna's father. But this time they'd been surprised by the fierce defenses of Toom and its surrounding neighbors.

But even so . . .

How in the name of Span and the clocks had *she* been summoned?

A powerful, velvet-throated voice echoed in the many-sided chamber, silencing the audience that swallowed up Renna. The sound sent a throbbing pulse through her sensitive Umbra cloak. The black cloth was attuned to her emotions and occasionally responded like a living thing.

"Greetings to you all," the Appon said. "I wish that you had gathered here today under better circumstances."

Renna was small and light—good traits for an Umbra Fighter—but it meant she had to stand on tiptoe to see the collective Appon, gathered in a semi-circle upon a dais. There were nine of them, each one tall and thin with long, straight hair tied back from their weathered faces. At first glance, she would've taken them for humans, especially since some were dark-skinned and some fair.

But they were too thin, too angular, and oddly jointed. And of course, their eyes were solid white and impossibly large. Each pair was a window into the collective knowledge of the Appon.

They were an ancient race with origins on turbulent Avid, the sister world of Span.

"As most of you know, a shapeshifting creature has infiltrated the Time Tower and managed to speed up the Avidian clock," the Appon continued. "Thankfully, it was destroyed by our vigilant Clock Keepers before it managed to sync the clocks and fully open the borders between our worlds. But our safety relies upon the clocks' resetting."

The frightened listeners murmured amongst themselves.

"How did this happen?" someone called out.

"This shifter took on the form of one Clock Keeper to fool the other," a pale Appon spoke up.

Renna shifted in her boots and glanced at the tense faces around her.

A thin, dark-haired figure near her was listening with a frown. He wore a sleeveless black shirt and a narrow sword hung from his wide-legged trousers. His long, pale arms were lightly feathered,

3

and she realized he was a Krimmer: a near-human, aerial species with hollow bones, wiry and lithe. He noticed her scrutiny and narrowed his bright green eyes. She looked away directly.

It was not the eye color of anyone back home in Toom. Like most of the villagers there, Renna had brown eyes that matched her skin and her short, curly hair. The small, silver hoop earrings peeking through the curls today were a gift from her mother, for luck. What she didn't know was how much they offset the deep blackness of her cloak and sparkled.

"This altering of Avid's clock has already allowed a small breach between our worlds," an Appon warned, and the crowd grew still, ears pricked. "We have received reports of Avidian beasts appearing in cities and villages—bursting from wells, springing from forest canopies."

"Fire beasts have attacked Luder!" someone shouted from the crowd.

"Spiked demons in Trivineen," another declared.

The assembly stirred in dismay, heads turning to demand details or share similar stories.

Their fear was certainly justified. For as long as anyone could remember, the Two Clocks had kept the worlds of Avid and Span apart, ensuring the safety of the one from the destructive and warring species of the other.

When the ancient Appon first escaped to Span, in a time that few races lived long enough to recall, they struggled desperately to find a way to keep the wild Avidian creatures from following them. Their astral powers had been strong enough to tear a hole between dimensions, allowing them to flee through it, but sealing it back up was beyond their abilities.

Until one among them, the quiet Elevad, designed and built two extraordinary clocks, set one hour apart: One kept the time in Avid and the other in Span. With the energy of Elevad's powerful astral spirit, the setting of the timepieces created a secure boundary between the worlds. But only so long as the clocks were never altered.

The effort was a success, but the strength it required took Elevad's life.

The story didn't end there, however. Many centuries later, still long before Renna was born, a power-hungry magician named Lugis found a way to sync the clocks, cracking open the border between Avid and Span. Then suddenly the world was filled with monstrous Avidian beasts that rose to his bidding.

It was shortly after that the Clock Keepers had been created by the Appon, with the help of the Scralls, who had been cataloging the "old magic" from Avid along with the magical properties of Span. The Clock Keepers were silent, single-purposed wizards, supposedly deathless and yet also barely alive.

Renna had wondered before if such a life might not grow unbearably weary for the Clock Keepers. But they went through the same motions daily in order to protect the clocks, and since that time, Span had been safe from Avid.

Until now.

"What will we do?" someone in the assembly cried out. "The days of champions like

Santir are over!"

It was Santir—a common Rydit blacksmith who possessed a secret talent for magic—who had fought the villain Lugis and destroyed him. The clocks were reset to one hour apart and the demons that had infiltrated Span were gradually rounded up and crushed.

Renna hunched her shoulders, the truth of those words settling into her bones like an ache. What was she doing here?

A deep-seated, old self-doubt swirled up in her stomach, encouraged by the fresh heartache from Callin's rejection back home. Callin, her dear childhood companion whom she discovered one day that she loved so much more than as a friend and sparring partner. But her feelings were not requited and his reaction to them was harsh, leaving Renna to crawl back inside herself in shame.

She was not good enough.

For the hundredth time, she thought the Appon must have made a mistake.

But the letter had been crimson and etched in golden ink, delivered by one of their servants. An official summons for Renna Estarlin of the village Toom. And Barrin, her teacher, had not seemed at all surprised. She wondered now if he had contacted the Appon about her.

"Can't the Clock Keepers reset the clocks?" someone asked from the crowd. Others made sounds of agreement.

"The Clock Keepers were designed so that they cannot alter their own charges. This was to prevent temptation, but perhaps it was unwise of us in the end," one of the Appon explained. "In a case such as this, they were meant to seal the tower with ancient magic to protect the clocks. This they have done and can't undo."

"A Scrall is the best individual to remove the seal and reset the clocks," an Appon with a sweet, clear voice declared. "Because we can no longer travel ourselves, old as we are, nor can we wield such magic in our astral forms. And a Scrall must be escorted there by a worthy team, skilled in combat and magic to protect against these new dangers reported across the land."

"The mayor-councils of Laribb, Ninder, Iddlar, and others have offered soldiers as escorts, but their armies are needed at home to protect their own people. That is why we've summoned a special group with gifts more relevant to this mission."

The assembly stirred curiously, listening.

"We have chosen our Scrall," the baritone Appon continued. "His name is Virallon Maggan. Virallon, step forward!"

Renna turned to see as the crowd shuffled and parted, making way for a diminutive figure. Outside of their exalted memories and historical knowledge, she knew only that Scralls were small and of the four-fingered folk, races that were more common when the Appon first arrived in Span.

Virallon was an old name and it suited: Frizzled gray and white hair spilled from his chin and out of his drooping black cap. Faded purple robes pooled around him as he came to a stop before the ring of Appon.

They regarded him with approval in their solid white eyes. Then he turned stiffly to face the assembly, revealing keen eyes of a startling yellow

7

color. His face was also amber, and swallowed up by wrinkles and a severe frown, without much nose to speak of.

"Virallon Maggan, outstanding among his people for his knowledge of the old magic, and his perseverance in all matters."

The crowd studied him in awe and Renna shifted her feet again, impatiently. Perseverance in *all* matters was not necessarily a positive trait, but she hoped that the Appon knew best.

"And now we shall call forth those summoned to accompany him to the Time Tower," the Appon announced, his words reverberating throughout the hall.

Renna's cloak crackled with nerves along her shoulders, and she squeezed her staff, attempting to remain calm.

"Dunn, the Huewit, of Mustin! Summoned for his power of vision."

A Huewit! Renna forgot her jitters for the moment and looked up eagerly as a distinctive figure strode forth from the back of the crowd. She had heard tales of the mystics who shared a kinship with deer, but never seen one.

A wide berth formed as a pair of massive antlers swept above the heads. Renna caught the gleam of large and luminous black eyes. The Huewit was very tall. He was golden skinned with brown fur on his limbs that matched the tawny hair falling to his shoulders. He wore a long, belted tunic that hung to his knees, his cloven hooves visible below. A large bow and quiver of arrows hung from his back.

"His gift of foresight—unusually strong

even among his kind—will be of great assistance on this mission."

Dunn bowed respectfully to the Appon and the Scrall, then turned his mesmerizing gaze out upon the assembly.

"Next, Trujo the Ralgir! Summoned from Alabass for his astounding strength."

Renna gasped as the massive Ralgir thumped his way to the forefront. Carrying an axe with a blade the size of her own torso, he was at least as tall as Dunn and broad as three men across. His limbs were like small tree trunks and his footfalls shook the floor beneath her feet as she stared. Wearing only trousers, he gave the impression of being all hairless, reddish-brown skin. Bald as an infant, his round face with its pointed nose and leering grin was offset by tapered ears.

As a small child, Renna had once seen a Ralgir traveling through Toom with a human companion. She had been terrified by its size and hidden like a mouse. That one had not been smiling, however.

"Hello there!" Trujo addressed the Appon.

Renna winced at his familiarity. A few of the wise ones glanced at each other, but their expressions were inscrutable. The Ralgir turned to thump his chest in salute to the crowd.

Several people in the hall chuckled and a soft cheer rose from a far corner. Good humor was not something Renna had expected, but she preferred it to Virallon's scowl.

The Krimmer next to Renna flinched as the Appon called out again to the assembly.

"Next is Lazzard Exlorid, the Krimmer!

From the vaulted city of Ninder."

So named, the Krimmer strode forth and joined the two giants and one tiny Scrall. Like them, he turned to face the assembly, but he wore a smug half-smile. Then he suddenly levitated, matching the height of his head with Trujo and Dunn's.

Renna couldn't help but giggle, especially since Virallon noticed and frowned.

"Lazzard is chosen for his skill in battle and knowledge of the sky hues," the Appon declared. The crowd murmured its approval.

Renna waited for her own name to ring out incongruously across the hall.

But she was not next. There was one other.

"Our fourth escort bears a name known to many of you," the sweet-voiced Appon informed the assembly. "We now call forth Sallindar the Tillen to join our chosen company."

Renna jerked in surprise, just as the people around her gasped and exclaimed to each other. The Tillen were so mysterious and reclusive that there were some back in Toom that denied their existence . . . despite the story of the one called Sallindar, who famously rescued the entire mountain city of Luftine from an avalanche. He had been passing through and came to their aid with the lightning speed of his kind.

But here he was now, treading soundlessly through the parting crowd. He was scarcely taller than Renna and appeared delicate at first glance, but he somehow emanated strength. It was like a golden aura around him. Four-fingered like Virallon, he had long, straight brown hair and narrow brown eyes in a thin, pale face. Other than a simple tunic and trousers like Renna's, he wore a necklace with a large silver pendant and a short sword strapped to his hip.

He joined the others and bowed his head to the Appon, as the assembly buzzed in excitement.

"Sallindar is chosen for his extraordinary skills as well as his exhibited compassion," the Appon told the assembly.

The Tillen's face belied the latter description: It was perfectly blank, even icy.

Then Renna's stomach lurched as she thought of what would surely come next. Any moment now, she must do the same as this famous individual—puny and obscure that she was.

"And lastly, to complete our team, we call upon Renna Estarlin of Toom," the Appon said. "A human."

A different kind of surprise rippled through the crowd. Renna closed her eyes, swallowing the bile that fought its way up her throat.

Old Barrin believed in her; her mother believed in her. And the Appon did not make mistakes.

She opened her eyes and walked carefully up to the dais, under the inquisitive stares of the other five. She heard the excited whispering behind her. Though roughly a quarter of the crowd were humans themselves, they had not expected one to be among those summoned today. Not unless it was some renowned wizard.

"Renna Estarlin was chosen for her superior skill in Umbra Combat."

The words seemed to float visibly in the air as she turned to face the assembly. It was dizzying

11

to see their faces gaping back at her. She gathered her restless black cloak with one shaky hand and clenched her staff with the other.

"These are our six champions!" the Appon cried out together.

Renna flinched and looked back at them in surprise. Trujo caught her eye from his great height and winked.

"They shall wear our emblem so that wherever the mission takes them, they may be received by all in good faith!"

A long-robed attendant approached the line of the summoned, carrying a case reverently before him. Renna watched as he opened it before Virallon the Scrall: Inside was a row of deep red badges like tiny hearts.

The badges were made of two crimson overlapping stones, representing Span and Avid. Superimposed at the center was a miniscule gold clock.

The attendant held up one of the badges as if to hand it to the Scrall. Then he paused and glanced at the Appon.

"When each of you accepts this important task and bears our emblem, you agree to see it through to the end, no matter the cost," the sweet-voiced ancient told them.

This was why the Appon had wanted them all to meet at the Observatory Hearth, to secure their promises and gift them with their symbol.

Renna held her breath, wondering what issues might arise that could make one of them abandon such a mission.

"Incline your head if you accept and agree,"

the Appon commanded.

She nodded numbly along with the others. Then the assembly cheered, their voices hurtling around the great room. The attendant gave each of the chosen a red badge, pressing Renna's into the palm of her hand. It was lighter than it appeared, but solid. She hurried to pin it onto her cloak like the others as the roar of the crowd continued.

It was official now. There was no turning back.

"The company will depart at dawn!" the Appon exclaimed over the noise. "And within three weeks' time, they shall meet with the Mands at Tindin, who have sworn to aid them if needed. May they travel with luck and speed."

Chapter Two

Renna approached the Observatory Hearth stables, stifling a yawn as the pale morning colors of the sky broke through. She had lain awake fretting for most of the night in the guest quarters, listening to what almost certainly had been the Ralgir snoring through the walls. And possibly the Scrall talking in his sleep.

The servants of the Appon were small, single-horned figures that bustled about, fitting the travelers' steeds with supplies. All but Lazzard had arrived before her, each with his red badge conspicuous on his clothing.

Unsurprisingly, Trujo's mount was not quite a horse, but an animal that Renna had never seen before: a significantly wider, shaggier, four-legged animal with no tail and very little mane. The Ralgir was patting its blunt, wide-eyed face gently. Dunn's horse was a large, brown stallion with a billowing mane, in contrast. The Scrall had been given a tan pony, but small as it was, the horned servants were fitting its saddle with descending stirrups so he could mount more easily.

Renna's heart swelled in reassurance as her dear gray-and-white horse Stalwart was led out to her, nicely groomed. He smelled of the stable and campfires at home as he snorted and stuffed his nose into her hands. No doubt he thought they were returning to Toom after one night in this strange place.

Standing off to one side, his ghost-white horse waiting quietly, was Sallindar the Tillen. His enigmatic gaze met Renna's and she looked away, intimidated—toward Dunn who sat adjusting the quiver on his back.

Her breakfast tumbled around in her stomach as she mounted Stalwart and steadied him. Her pack filled with travel-bread, a bedroll, and a water pouch was strapped behind her, and her hickory staff was in its sheath across her back.

"It's time we were off," Virallon spoke. "Where is the Krimmer?" He squinted at the rest of them with disapproving yellow eyes.

"Let's hope he didn't have a change of heart," Trujo said. "He's our navigator."

The Krimmer's black horse stood waiting patiently, its horned attendant looking up at the sky.

"We all know the general direction." Dunn's voice rang musically through the open air. Renna's ears pricked up at the sound, and she thought of Tannir back home, the village's best singer.

"I can't read all those changing colors," the Ralgir said, gesturing up at the sky.

Most of the patterns of sky hues varied with the weather and the season, but several formations remained fixed, allowing travelers to use them as guides. They were streaks of purples, greens, and golds, splashed across the blue dome. The night sky hues—mostly blues and whites—were the only source of light in the darkness.

"Anyway, we can't leave behind one of the champions," Trujo added with a toothy smile.

Virallon huffed from his small horse.

"I'm surprised the Appon used that word. As if this ragtag crew compared to Santir and his magic. The days of such heroes are over," he said, echoing the crowd from the day before.

"I beg to differ!" Lazzard's voice floated over their heads.

Renna looked up as he sailed above them, turned a neat somersault in the air, and settled lightly onto his horse. The animal only shifted for a moment, apparently used to such behavior.

"*I'm* feeling heroic this morning, despite oversleeping." Lazzard flashed a smile and Renna wondered if he'd been late on purpose, just to make such an entrance.

Virallon snorted, gathering his reins. "Do you suppose, young Krimmer, that any champion of old truly felt himself to be heroic?"

Lazzard frowned at his tone.

"Or was it simply inherent in them? Born of a sense of purpose and serious disposition?" Virallon demanded.

"I don't know, decrepit Scrall. I've never been able to ask one."

Trujo chortled at that and Virallon's lined face darkened.

"Make no mistake, we are a poor excuse for those who went before us," the scholar admonished them all. "Let no one allow himself to puff up with pride or vanity on this most important undertaking."

Renna's heart sank at his words. She hadn't

16

expected such a lack of faith from the one whose knowledge was supposed to carry them all.

Lazzard's face turned red, as if the words "pride or vanity" had hit their mark. He sneered at Virallon and snapped back, "I don't care what the Appon says you can do. You better mind your tongue, you old fool."

Virallon bristled. "How dare you speak to me that way? I will—"

Dunn suddenly rode between them, cutting off his retort. He lowered his fierce rack of antlers at the Krimmer.

Renna squeezed Stalwart's reins. Were they splintering apart already? Virallon had been rude, but Lazzard's temper was a surprise—a sharp contrast to his careless humor.

"I dislike arguments," Dunn warned them both.

Lazzard eyed his antlers and nodded in submission.

"And so this one ends!" He turned to Virallon with a sardonic smile. "My apologies."

"Whether or not we compare to champions of old, we have been summoned for this task by the Appon," Dunn reminded the Scrall sternly. "They can only expect us to do our best."

"I hope that's true," Renna said quietly.

"A Ralgir always does his best!" Trujo declared.

Virallon turned indignantly to Sallindar, as if expecting him to take his side. But if the Tillen felt that the company of travelers was lacking, he said nothing of it. He met Virallon's gaze with stony silence until the Scrall turned away

17

uncomfortably.

"Then we have wasted too much time already. Let us be off!" he cried out.

At his kick, the pony sprang ahead, trotting toward the single road that led to and from the Observatory Hearth. The others followed, overtaking the small horse rapidly. Dunn and Lazzard moved into the lead and Sallindar took up the rear near Renna.

She glanced back at the great dome behind them, knowing the Appon were surely watching them go with the aid of the Avidian stone. The stable workers saluted her and she waved, responsibility settling like wooden beams upon her shoulders.

What would happen if they failed? Would the Appon summon a new team and try again? She refused to think of the terrible letter that would arrive at Toom if she did not survive.

The company rode in silence as the day colors broke out in full, light flaring across the lush fields that surrounded the Observatory Hearth. Renna admired the gold shining upon the green and the small herds of grazing animals that raised their heads as they passed.

Life thrilled her the way it only did when she was in Umbra Combat: cloaked in the shadow generated by her cloak, her staff spinning like a branch caught in a maelstrom.

The situation might be dire, but here was also an adventure—one that had taken her away from her troubles back home.

"Look at the way the human rides," Trujo said suddenly.

Renna almost looked around for another human before she realized that he meant her.

"Leaning over like she's never been in a saddle before," he went on as if she couldn't hear.

She frowned, sitting up straight on Stalwart's back.

"I've ridden horseback my whole life," she told him.

"That is the way humans ride," Dunn said in his melodious voice. "Have you never interacted with them before?"

The Ralgir shook his head, wiggling his pointed ears.

"Nor have I," Virallon said, disinterested.

"Why are you speaking as if I'm not here?" Renna asked, bewildered.

"I, on the other hand, have had several affairs with them," Lazzard said with a satisfied air. He leered at Renna and she bridled, the blood rushing to her cheeks. She wasn't surprised by this declaration, however, given his striking looks.

She thought of Callin for a single instant and the soreness in her heart throbbed.

"Let us speak no more of *that*," Virallon said in a disgusted tone.

Renna's temper flared. "Let us speak no more as if a human were not right here," she snapped.

Only Sallindar seemed to hear her, regarding her quietly.

"Are they this awkward at everything?" Trujo asked.

Lazzard tilted his head to consider. "Not *every*thing—"

"As if Ralgirs are graceful!" Renna exploded at Trujo. "And not great, clumsy louts!"

She bit her tongue immediately, as all heads turned to stare in surprise. Trujo's broad face twisted into an intimidating scowl, but Renna forced herself to glare back at him. It might have been dangerous to risk his anger, but she couldn't allow them all to think she was afraid. Or inferior because she was human.

"Someone's risking the wrath of the Heuwit with that tone of voice," Lazzard said, amused.

"I can insult you all, if that's what makes you listen," she said, sticking her chin out. But she sounded childish to her own ears and regretted it.

Lazzard cackled with laughter. She cringed as he floated up from his saddle with his head thrown back. Virallon rolled his eyes.

Trujo's face cleared at the laughter. He grinned at Renna unexpectedly, revealing teeth that were each the size of her eye. She smiled back despite the fierce sight.

"Are they feisty and foolish as well?" he asked Lazzard, pointedly still pretending she wasn't there.

"We are," Renna admitted, just as Sallindar said, "They are."

There was a startled pause at the unfamiliar sound of his speech. He had a sandy-throated voice, soft but with a slight rasp.

Renna gave him a quick glance, unsure whether he'd just insulted her. But he was frowning ahead into the distance, his mind seemingly on something else.

Another human, perhaps—from his past.

"The fact that human numbers are so small is testament alone of that," Virallon said.

"It is *not*," Renna snapped. "As a Scrall, you should be well aware that the Coddant War wiped out a third of my kind."

"Indeed," Dunn spoke up. He dipped his antlers in sympathy. "The Coddants' use of destructive weather in their war was irresponsible and shameful."

His words eased the tension in Renna's shoulders. The Coddants were a hawk-like race whose elders could summon wind and the rain, and their territorial disputes had lasted a decade. The stories of the terrible storms and floods in that period, only thirty years before Renna was born, were legion even in her tiny village—blessedly far from the destruction.

Now the Coddants lived high up in the Cold Mountains, above the mostly human city of Luftine, under a pact for peace.

Virallon turned to scowl back at Renna. "History does not hold the Coddants accountable for the suffering of your fragile species," he said with a sniff.

"*Human* history does," she retorted.

"Everyone has their own version of history," Lazzard said darkly. He had settled back onto his horse and began pulling out maps from his pack.

"The Appon possess what is considered to be the official account in the vaults of the Observatory Hearth," Dunn reminded him and Virallon nodded.

"Who says it's official?" Lazzard asked.

"Who says?" the Scrall hooted. "Detailed,

neutral records of the history of Span are constantly preserved by the Appon—"

"No history is official unless it says Ralgirs are the biggest and the best," Trujo said with a hearty chuckle.

Renna had to smile at that silliness, even as Lazzard groaned.

Thunder rumbled distantly and she glanced ahead at the sky. Purple and gold panels of color reflected on the gathering clouds, creating patches of brilliance and shadow. She reached behind her to dig for her rain cloak, holding tight to Stalwart's reins. He was alert and eager, his ears and nose twitching to catch the new sounds and smells, which now included fresh rain.

They were headed for a valley lined with spidery trees, crooked branches interlocked and furry.

"My kind has always strived to keep an unbiased record of history," Sallindar said suddenly, breaking the short silence. It didn't sound like a boast or argument, just a statement.

Shaking out one of his maps, Lazzard glanced at Sallindar sideways with his green eyes.

"We'll have to take your word for that, won't we, Tillen? As secretive as your kind are."

Sallindar said nothing, apparently unoffended.

The first drops of rain began to fall as they descended into the valley. By nightfall, it had become a deluge and the riding was a miserable slosh through the muddy road. The horses and Trujo's steed splashed reluctantly forward, while Virallon's pony was practically swimming.

Stalwart was indignant that they continued onward. He kept turning his large head back to appeal to Renna to stop. She shook her own head back at him, not willing to be the one who slowed the team down.

Several miserable hours later, Dunn called out and pointed to a thick cluster of the furry trees, signaling a stop. Renna's teeth were chattering, and her muscles clenched with the cold. She blew out her breath in relief, steering Stalwart off the flooded road.

The group of horses slipped and slid into the dubious shelter, while Trujo's mount simply crashed its way through, letting out deep grunts as it went.

It was dark under the trees, but the ground wasn't nearly as wet underfoot. The animals grazed unhappily in the mushy grass. Renna slid down into the soft mud and threw back her drenched rain cloak, shivering.

"Where is a Coddant elder when you need one?" Lazzard grumbled.

"This is costing us valuable time," Virallon said, huddled atop his exhausted pony. "But I suppose drowning in the saddle helps no one."

"It's time to eat anyway," Trujo said, and swung his big bulk down to the ground.

"I'll make a fire," Sallindar offered, dropping lightly to his feet.

Renna and the others looked at him in surprise.

"It is too damp for a fire, Tillen," Dunn stated the obvious.

Sallindar ignored him and crouched down in

a graceful, catlike manner, slinging his pack around to his front.

"If your kind has elemental magic," Lazzard told him. "Then perhaps you could stop this downpour?"

Sallindar shook his head.

"Of course not." Lazzard dismounted and leaned against his horse with a yawn.

Sallindar poured some fine grains from a small pouch onto the ground and spread them out with his hands. Virallon watched keenly, reminding Renna that even the Scrall knew little about the Tillen. His movements were extremely light and efficient.

"Bring me the driest branches you can find," he said, glancing up at Trujo and Renna.

"I will do some foraging to add to our dampened food supplies," Dunn said and pulled his bow from his shoulder. Hunting in the rain was not likely to be easy either, but he seemed the most capable for the task.

Renna did the best she could with the water-logged wood around them. Trujo contributed by snapping off a large branch and breaking it into smaller bits.

Sallindar waited a few moments and then gathered back up the dust from the ground as carefully as he could. He patted the dirt underneath afterwards and said matter-of-factly, "It's dry now."

"What?" Renna stared and Lazzard flashed him a skeptical look.

Sallindar took the damp wood and arranged it on the ground. Then he sprinkled more of his strange drying powder over them. He struck a match, as Trujo whistled in disbelief.

"Is it really dry?" Renna asked, crouching to see.

He answered by lighting the kindling and blowing on the ensuing smoke. There was slippery mud all around his fire, but the center burned with ease.

"How in the name of Span?" Trujo asked.

"Dust of the Cartru Desert," Virallon announced, impressed. "A powerfully absorbent substance. I had thought there was none left."

"So it's not some mysterious magic," Lazzard said, leaning back against his horse. "Does this mean you can make us dry beds for the night?"

Sallindar shook his head again.

"It's an extremely rare substance and you want him to use it to make you a bed?" Virallon snorted.

"What better purpose for it?" Lazzard taunted him.

Renna grinned. "I'm happy just to have a fire."

Shortly afterward, the company gathered around their unlikely hearth, roasting a shaggy hog that Dunn had dragged back from his excursion. The Heuwit himself ate large handfuls of plants that he'd gathered, since his deer-like race did not eat meat.

Renna was grateful for the rest, especially after her light sleep the night before. She knew that most of the days ahead would be much longer and harder. If one rode without stopping—an impossible task—the journey to the Time Tower was roughly two weeks. They would be exposed to all kinds of weather, and they had to cut through the dense Aggard Forest. Along the way, some places would need protection from the type of attacks described at the Observatory Hearth.

"So Virallon, how do you intend to crack the spell on the Time Tower?" Lazzard asked, interrupting Renna's thoughts.

The Scrall wiped some grease from his lips and then smacked them together with satisfaction.

"The actual spell is beyond your capacity to understand," he replied. Lazzard snorted. "But I can tell you that both the seal and its removal are very old magic from Avid, before the days of Lugis and Santir."

"Can you explain the difference between old and new magic?" Dunn asked, gazing at Virallon with his sensitive eyes. "My kind have had 'the sight' since we first evolved, but I sense that this may not be old enough to qualify."

"Indeed, most of the magic possessed in this world is still fairly new. The magic of old is heavily influenced by the powerful forces of Avid," Virallon explained, his own eyes brightening as he spoke. "It is that mysterious essence that Elevad of the Appon used to forge the clocks."

"But Lugis was still able to sync them," Lazzard said with his mouth full. "Assuming it's not all just a legend."

"Just a legend?" Virallon gaped at him.

"Well, it's never been *proven*, has it?" the Krimmer said mildly.

Renna gave him a surprised glance. No one had ever spoken about Lugis and Santir around *her* as if the tale might not be fact.

"There is a vast wealth of documentation!" the Scrall exclaimed.

"I know Lugis was a powerful magician," Trujo chimed in, picking at his teeth. "What do you call it? An Extru-something? Extru-krim?"

"Extrunikrim," Renna said automatically. "Like Umbra Nox."

That long-ago human had possessed the power of invisibility and uncanny physical prowess. But instead of turning it toward a dark purpose, he had started an informal academy in Iddlar to teach others how to tap into a similar state of being, creating the Umbra Combat tradition, passed down through many generations. Umbra cloaks and the best hickory staffs were still made only at the original Nox academy, ordered far and wide by messenger.

"So, he had some of that old magic," Trujo added.

"Extrunikrim are extraordinary, often dangerous, individuals," Virallon said. "It's a blessing that they are so rare. As far as we know, they've all been the offspring of already powerful magical parents, usually those who were unable to reproduce for quite some time before."

In all the renderings of Lugis, the villain had skin of the deepest blue and he was powerfully muscular, almost like Trujo. He had been a hybrid of several species, but no one knew for sure which ones. He was bearded with a face like a human, but he possessed a long, forked tail. One other distinguishing trait was the pair of small, skeletal wings on his back.

"It's unusual that he was a hybrid species

and an Extrunikrim," Renna mused aloud.

"He was quite the freak of nature," Lazzard muttered.

"But there were many new hybrids in those days," Dunn reminded her. "When the Appon first arrived, some Avidian species came with them, and they bred with the ones in Span. It is how my people first originated."

"Not Ralgirs," Trujo said with satisfaction. "We're all Span! No taint from Avid."

"Humans too," Renna added. "That's why we rarely have any magic."

"A dubious distinction," Lazzard said drily.

"Yet early Scralls were native too," Dunn pointed out.

"My ancestors were highly receptive and absorbed much from the Appon," Virallon said proudly, resettling himself on the damp blanket that was his seat by the fire. "But you must understand, Lugis was psychologically disturbed. With his power, he could've destroyed every mayor-council and made himself a mighty king, one that ruled over every region, but that was not enough for him. He wanted to harness the chaos of Avid."

The Scrall's words painted images among the flames and dancing sparks in the darkness. His golden eyes were eerie as well, and goosebumps rose on Renna's arms as he spoke.

"And in those days, the clocks were protected only by ordinary guards—powerful ones like Ralgirs, to be sure, and magicians of the usual standard." Virallon said this last part with a sniff. "No one ever truly imagined that someone would be foolhardy or sinister enough to try to tamper with them. It was an immense lapse of judgement." He fell silent a moment.

"So Lugis vanquished these guards and then used old magic to sync the clocks?" Lazzard asked.

"But first he stopped at Santir's blacksmith shop to have a scepter made, and it raised his suspicions," Renna recounted.

"Yes, Santir." Virallon shook his gray head in awe for a moment. "No one knows how he possessed such a strong spark of magic. None of his kind ever had it before or had it since."

"As far as *we* know," Sallindar replied.

That was what people meant when they said that such heroes no longer existed. Rydits were solidly built, four-armed creatures that were inclined toward heavy labor and recreational combat. But Santir had carried a secret talent for a rare form of magic: the casting of a protective shield around oneself. It was the kind of barrier that could only be penetrated from the inside out. Santir's had been so solid that even an Extrunikrim could not break it. Or at least, a surprised and unprepared one.

"As you know, Santir surprised Lugis in the Time Tower, shielded himself, and killed him. Then the Appon, at that time still strong enough to travel, reset the clocks themselves. One can't even move the clocks' hands without knowledge of ancient magic."

Renna stared at the Scrall as his words sunk in.

"But then how was this shapeshifter able to do it?" she asked.

"I don't know," he said reluctantly. His

brows furrowed into a dark V. "It would seem that he holds some small store of old magic."

"What do we know of this demon?" Dunn asked. "Where did he come from?"

"And how do we know he was male?" Renna muttered. She had often reminded Callin not to assume that powerful figures weren't female.

Lazzard rolled his eyes at her.

"Nothing is known. Whatever his story is, it was blasted into particles along with his body by our valiant Clock Keepers," Virallon declared.

The company was silent as the fire crackled. Renna wondered what kind of power this shapeshifter truly had . . . And if it could be destroyed that easily.

"Perhaps they should have asked it some questions first," Sallindar said.

Chapter Three

Several long hours passed before the storm abated, during which the travelers rested as best as they could. Then they rode out into the dark night, the damp air chilling Renna to the bone beneath her cloak. Stalwart shook out his mane in a shivery motion and snorted a gust of steam.

Lazzard seemed to delight in the frigid air, flying up ahead with his eyes raised to the brilliant night sky colors. Dunn caught hold of Lazzard's horse and led it along with his own, watching the Krimmer spin slowly in the air.

"The Great Kenda is back in view tonight!" Lazzard called, citing the blue, wheel-shaped pattern most prevalent in the sky. "We can follow it without trouble. But the Ren Set is out of its normal rotation now."

"That's my namesake, the Ren Set," Renna said with chattering teeth.

"That is lucky, to be sky hue-named," Dunn told her.

"Not for humans," Lazzard declared. He drifted back toward them as Renna glared at him. "And there's the Winged Alka formation." He raised an eyebrow at Sallindar. "Named after a race

31

most familiar to our Tillen companion."

"Oh ho, that's right! I heard he led the defense against the Alka, the ones that wanted Tillen land." Trujo swung his head around to grin at Sallindar.

The Tillen regarded him a moment and then nodded.

The Alka were a free-spirited race of serpents with latticed wings that frequently moved their territories.

"Shot them all out of the sky, the story goes! With a borrowed bow." Trujo whistled and steered his giant mount away from a stone in the road. "The bow's not even your natural weapon, is it?"

Sallindar just shook his head.

"He's not much of a conversationalist either," Lazzard said with a snort.

"Not everyone is a braggart," Virallon shot at him.

"Yes, Scralls are surpassingly humble," Lazzard mocked him, settling back onto his horse. "But look up ahead! We're approaching Gwin, where we're sure to find some entertaining, wagging tongues."

He waved an arm toward the dark horizon, where Renna could just make out the tiny lights of the town.

"We shouldn't stop," she said, wishing they could. A warm bed would have been a wondrous thing.

"Certainly not for conversation! We can skirt it," Virallon declared, although he shivered dispiritedly.

"No," Dunn spoke up, surprising them.

A distant, dreamy expression had fallen over his face. He dropped his reins and gazed out into the night.

"No," he repeated. "We are needed."

Everyone stared at him, waiting.

"The people of Gwin . . . are in danger."

There was only a moment's hesitation. Then everyone kicked their mounts into action.

Here we go, Renna thought, and her heart flew out into the night before them. Hooves struck the dirt road in a thunderous chorus as they raced toward the town ahead.

Whatever happened next—whether she proved herself or fell into shame—at least it would not be before the Appon and a wide-ranging assembly.

Before long, scattered houses with thatched roofs were flying past them in the outskirts of the town. Then the gate was before them, decked with crude insignia and symbols of Gwin's prominent families.

Renna drew up Stalwart breathlessly and waited. Everything was quiet in the darkness, lit only by a pair of dim lamps set into the gate.

"Are we too late?" Trujo asked.

A moment after he spoke, the entryway creaked open, making them all jump. It flapped back and forth in a breeze, revealing a distinct lack of guards to whom they might have shown their Appon badges.

Sallindar rode forward and slipped through as silently as a ghost. The others followed with stealth, although Stalwart let out a nervous snort as Renna guided him through. On the other side, the town lay hushed and dark—except for a strange droning, wheezing sound. It was like the humming of bees intermingled with the snores of a giant. Or a great many giants.

And then came the stench, as if a thousand dead things and piles of dung had been turned over at once.

"What is that?" Virallon hissed from behind.

Renna covered her nose and followed Dunn and Trujo as they circled their mounts, peering into the darkness in all directions. She caught sight of a mass above the thatched roofs, not fifty feet from the gate. Sallindar was already gazing at it: a mysterious mound in the midst of the town, rising and falling in place ever so slightly.

"Spinners," he whispered, surprised.

Renna glanced at the others, unfamiliar with the name. Lazzard floated up off his horse for a better look.

"Ugh, disgusting beetle-things," he reported. "There's a mountain of them sleeping in their own dung and trash."

"I heard about Spinner attacks when I was a Ralgir tot," Trujo said, ears wiggling. "But they were supposed to be wiped out long ago."

Virallon nodded. "These rolled through a rift created by the altered clocks, like the other reported Avidian creatures."

"Everyone must have run away, surely," Renna said, looking back at the unlocked gate.

"No." The Heuwit listened, angling his ears toward the nearby houses. "Many are hiding, afraid to wake the Spinners."

Sallindar nodded in agreement, his own

hearing just as sharp.

"I'm not afraid to wake them," Trujo said with a grin.

"We do not want to scatter them all over the town," Dunn told him.

"Let us take a closer look," Virallon said, riding forward.

Renna and the others followed, hooves thudding softly on the ground. The Spinners' sleeping noises grew louder. When they came into full view, she gasped at the putrid stench up close.

They were indeed like giant, black beetles—their shells the size of cottage roofs—stacked haphazardly upon each other in a slovenly heap. It was more like a nest than any kind of camp, with shreds of trash, dung, and rotting food wedged in between their shells. Their jointed, spiny limbs sprawled across each other and dangled toward the ground.

Yet all around the disgusting, stinking mound there was a shimmering aura. Even in the dark, Renna could see a prism-like effect in the air between them and the Spinners' bodies.

"How could these oversized insects cast a protective shield?" Lazzard asked, hand over his nose.

"This is no shield," Virallon scoffed. "It's a veneer created by their tiny strains of magic combined. I can dispel it with a simple charm."

The Scrall pulled on his beard a moment as the others struggled not to breathe in the stench. Then he held out his small, withered hand to Dunn.

Renna took the opportunity to study his four fingers a moment—something she had rarely seen back home. The little finger was the one missing, it seemed, with the rest of them spaced evenly.

"Heuwit, I require an arrow," he commanded.

Dunn blinked in hesitation, as if unwilling to part with any of his arsenal. But then he placed one arrow across the tiny palm.

Virallon studied the weapon a moment and murmured to himself. His eyes widened and grew brighter yellow. Renna stared as the arrow levitated and flashed for an instant in the darkness. Then it dropped back into his hand and his eyes faded. He nodded, looking back up at the others.

"This arrow should pierce the veneer and collapse it. But then the vermin will certainly wake," he warned.

Each of them drew their weapons. Renna slid down off Stalwart and closed her eyes a moment, drawing inward all her focus, all her conscious thought. That initial step in Umbra Combat had been the hardest to learn, but now it was innate. Her psychic connection with her cloak surged into the forefront and she pulled up her hood.

Adrenaline spiked with doubt and hope combusted inside her. The familiar voltage blasted through her veins and crackled in her hair. Her cloak flared outward like bat wings and then—she faded into a shadow.

It was only then she noticed that the others were watching. She took in their appraisal in the calm, neutral manner she had cultivated in training, but somewhere in the back of her mind, she was pleased.

Then Dunn fired the charmed arrow. It pierced the glistening air before them and sank into a Spinner's exposed shoulder joint. In a flash, its massive eyes cracked open, the whites brilliant in the dark. Then it exploded into a fury of writhing, snapping the others awake.

Trujo gave a roar as the nest collapsed into a rolling mess of black beetle bodies and limbs. More arrows from Dunn flew into the sprawl at once, just as Trujo charged forward on his steed, cracking the shells with his axe.

Renna set her teeth and spun like a wraith into their midst, crushing limbs and hulls with her staff. The Spinners leapt away from her in astonishment—they could barely see her, much less keep up with her blows. As she fought, she kept an eye out for her companions: Lazzard was swooping in and stabbing the demons underneath their shells; bolts of white light came from Virallon, shattering exoskeletons into dust.

They were outnumbered, but each of them could handle several Spinners at once. Now that the creatures had broken apart, it was clear that there were different sizes. Most were enormous, but some were small enough to be thrown by the others, their teeth and claws tearing through the air.

One such Spinner ball sliced into Trujo's arm, but he just snarled and crushed it with his fist. Another came flying toward Dunn, but Sallindar leapt into the air and caught it. He hurtled it back and it barreled through a Spinner's hull as if shot by a catapult.

Stunned, Renna almost lost her focus. The Tillen fought like he was dancing, like he was made

37

of liquid. Every limb struck a blow as often as his short sword pierced flesh. Every blow was graceful but punishing. Then he would leap as before and come crashing down upon the back of an escaping Spinner, driving his blade into one of its vulnerable eyes.

The sounds of cracking and crushing filled the air, along with grunts and the occasional shriek of a dying Spinner. It lasted for no more than twenty minutes—then abruptly, it was over.

The mound of beetles was gone, replaced by a field of detritus, stinking even worse than before.

Renna sighed and let her muscles go slack, her staff drooping toward her boots. She shook back her hood and allowed her focus to soften.

Barrin had called the Umbra state another realm, one that existed only inside the mind. But all she really knew was that it was her saving grace in combat, her special advantage, where others might have more strength or stamina.

She looked at her companions now as her cloak settled around her.

Lazzard was examining the bottom of his boot in disgust; a string of yellow Spinner guts stretched from his sole to the ground. Virallon was shaking his head contemptuously from his saddle. Trujo splashed water from a pouch over his sliced arm while Dunn gathered his spent arrows. There was gore on his antlers, a reminder that he would be formidable even if he lost his bow.

"Ho there, Sallindar!" Trujo called out. "I like your style on the battlefield."

The Tillen nodded and wiped his blade clean. He sheathed it and, without warning, cast his unsettling gaze upon Renna. Blood rushed to her face, and she dropped her eyes to the ground.

She reached out to settle Stalwart who had come tripping back to her after the battle. She had trained him long ago to run for cover in combat, since she didn't fight on horseback.

"I'm not sure he's lived up to the legends yet, but it *was* impressive," Lazzard muttered. He had resorted to scraping the guts from his boot with a dagger.

"The human fights well too," Trujo added, noticing Sallindar's look.

"Indeed. I have never seen an Umbra Fighter become so nearly invisible," Dunn remarked, and Renna's face burned with pride.

A short battle with simple creatures like Spinners was no proof yet that the Appon had chosen the right Umbra Fighter, but she welcomed any praise from the others. Somewhere inside her, a tiny part of the wound left by Callin was eased.

"I am only human," she said with a small smile.

Callin had been fierce in combat as well as she, although with a sword as his chosen weapon. To him, training to be unstoppable had been all-consuming. They both had dreamed of joining a company of soldiers and traveling the world, but there was no room for love in the version that Callin imagined for himself. In fact, he saw it as a sign of weakness and scorned it.

Renna's thoughts rushed back to the present as doors in the nearby houses began creaking open. A few residents of Gwin looked out at them silently, warily. It was clear that they weren't certain whether to thank their rescuers or run from them. But more and more emerged and stared at them.

The townsfolk were a mix of willowy, long-snouted Klydeers and four-legged, knob-shelled Idgians, as well as Rydits.

"They killed the Spinners!" came the mutterings.

"Did you *see* how they fought?"

"Who are they?"

Virallon unpinned his badge, cleared his throat, and held the emblem aloft.

"We are emissaries of the Appon, on our way to reset the Two Great Clocks," he announced, pride rumbling in his voice.

The people murmured to each other in awe and stared at the crimson badge.

"Those monsters appeared out of thin air!" someone called out. "Have the clocks been synced?"

"No," Dunn told them, hushing the voices with his deep tone. "But the Avidian time was changed."

"Better be on your guard for more of this havoc though," Trujo said cheerfully. "Until we get things fixed."

"Trujo!" Renna reproached him under her breath. The Gwinians were shaken up enough without that warning.

Now they sprang to action, darting back into their houses and slamming the doors shut. Lazzard folded his arms and glared at the Ralgir.

"We *might* have enjoyed a little grateful hospitality."

Trujo shrugged and looked apologetic.

"We've no time for gratitude, Krimmer," Virallon retorted. "We must move on."

*   *   *

Skink listened to the hawks screeching outside the Time Tower, his tail curled around his head. His inky-blue body was damp and slick against the smooth stone floor, regenerated from a tiny piece of flesh that had escaped the Clock Keepers' assault. His body was also crammed without dignity beneath the lowest edge of a ceiling-to-floor woodworking in the clock chamber.

He scowled at such cowering from the simple-minded Clock Keepers. But their power— limited as it was—could not be beaten. Not even his idol, Lugis, could have withstood the destruction of two Clock Keepers' full defensive force.

There had to be another way. If he was going to follow in Lugis's footsteps, Skink would have to use his wiles instead.

He watched Elix shrewdly as the Clock Keeper paced in front of his precious charges. The silent one's hands clutched the sides of his head as if he were miming despair. His face, like his partner Anderin's, was perfectly expressionless.

Skink could taste the emotions floating off him: restlessness, loneliness. A desperate need for escape from his monotonous existence. Skink licked the salty tang of it from his lips, intrigued. Perhaps the Keepers were not such simple beings after all.

Elix turned slowly and walked toward the closest window in the chamber. He placed a bone-white hand upon the glass in longing.

41

The shapeshifter watched him and debated the risk, wincing at the pain in his limbs from his contorted position. He decided that Lugis would have taken any chance. Indeed, he had taken a thousand chances, all those years ago.

"You feel trapped," Skink growled softly.

Elix flinched as if struck. He whirled and stared at the coiled blue beast sliding out from its hiding place. The Keeper's hand flew out, sparks crackling.

"Wait!" Skink rasped. "I have something you want!"

Half-exposed, he waited for the painful blast. But it did not come. Elix stared at him, unmoving, his fingers still alight.

Skink purred cautiously, slithering fully into view, his joints and muscles aching.

"Old magic that can change your destiny," he promised. "That's what you want, isn't it?"

Elix watched as Skink straightened himself out and offered a reptilian grin.

"Let me live, dear friend, and I will give you *exactly* what you want."

Chapter Four

They rode for two days without incident, taking shelter wherever they could by the banks of streams and in abandoned barns, creeping ever closer toward the dark green line of the Aggard Forest. Renna slept hard inside her bedroll, which she had knitted to be as warm as possible. The lingering smells of her own cottage—candles and straw, porridge and tea—were rapidly replaced by the thick, smoky odor of the campfires. Never had she been so tired and dirty.

And never had she spent so much time among non-humans. She caught herself studying her companions as stealthily as possible.

She noticed that Dunn's patches of fur shone like silk in the sunlight and his long, pointed face was often composed in deep thought. His hooves and bent legs gave him an awkward, staggering stride, but when he sat, he was motionless and quiet.

Trujo was the real outlier, of course, broad and thick as a cottage wall. His exposed ruddy torso revealed how craggy and tough his skin was, like animal hide that had been dried in the sun. His fingernails were thick, brown slabs and there was not a hair visible on him.

Lazzard's arm feathers were rough and bristly when he passed her a portion of meat by the fire. His nose and chin were sharp in an avian way, but still very human. He was restless like a bird, however, making quick movements and tilting his head.

He caught her gaze and scowled at her furiously. She looked away at first, flustered, but then she glared back, wondering why he was so angry. This time he winked at her and leered, suddenly flirtatious. She blushed, confused, and turned her back.

A memory of Callin's eyes materialized for a moment. His were a calm hazel, not glittering green and mocking.

She thought of something a friend had told her long ago: that she was a "straight arrow." She never paid special attention to anyone, or used whatever wiles she might possess, unless her intentions came from the heart. Playful types like Lazzard—even when they weren't ill-tempered—had always confused her a great deal.

What was the point of pretending to be interested in someone? Or attracting someone only to reject them? Whether it came from spite or boredom, she had no patience for it. She was hopelessly sincere.

Of the two four-fingered champions, the disgruntled Virallon was very like a human dwarf, except for his yellow eyes and miniscule nose. With his deep-set wrinkles, she imagined that he was quite old, even though he kept up with the others well enough. At night, he sometimes grew suddenly exhausted, and would drift off before he'd finished eating. Then he would murmur in his sleep.

Finally, there was Sallindar, who often seemed ephemeral, as if he might flicker in and out of view. It confused Renna that anyone could appear fragile and ethereal yet be fiercely strong.

He sometimes sat apart from the group and held his necklace pendant in his hand, his sharp eyes lost in thought. It was an oddly shaped silver emblem, a circle with a cluster of smaller ones inside. From his expression in those moments, she imagined it allowed him to see something far away, something that concerned him.

No one knew exactly where the Tillen lived, but they were said to keep to uninhabited forest lands. Sometimes a village of theirs would be discovered only to abruptly move away. They were few in number and kept to themselves, so it was unusual if Sallindar had traveled to the Cartru Desert to gather supplies like the drying dust.

Perhaps he was a loner that often ventured out to see the world.

Renna recalled that he had not spoken in their earlier conversation about hybrids and creatures native to Span. She wondered if the Tillen were something else altogether.

*   *   *

When at last they reached the Aggard Forest, Renna was taken back by the size of the trees. Hundreds of years old, they seemed to groan as they reached for the overcast sky, their limbs bulbous, bent, and twisted.

Ravens wheeled overhead and called to each

other, staring down at the company of riders at the entrance to the woods. Horned bats clustered high up in the branches, stirring their skeletal wings.

The hairs on the back of Renna's neck rose slowly to attention. Stalwart snorted and sidestepped, unsure how he felt about entering.

There was something uncanny here—not frightening, exactly, but strange.

The others were quiet, sensing it too, as Lazzard shuffled through his maps. Virallon whispered something to himself and made a small swirl motion with his fingers. Renna wondered if he were testing the air for some malignant forces.

Regardless of the eerie atmosphere, the closeness of the trees and the dense undergrowth made the woods appear impenetrable.

"There is supposed to be a hidden trail," Lazzard said, drifting off his horse and studying a map.

"The Oxtar Passage, first cleared over five hundred years ago by the Luderins," Virallon announced.

"The very one," Lazzard said, irritated. "I would have refused to set foot upon it without that background history."

"What do we need a trail for? Why don't we just smash our way through?" Trujo asked.

Virallon and Dunn looked at him aghast.

"We will not smash our way through an ancient and beautiful forest," the Scrall snapped.

"Not all of it. Just a few branches," Trujo insisted.

"The first Trivineen council mysteriously lost half its party traveling through this wood, never to be found," Virallon told him. "We will pass through it with *caution*."

Renna looked up again at the trees, her stomach knotting.

Sallindar dismounted silently and closed the distance between them and the first tree trunks on foot.

"The passage is hidden to the untrained eye, but there are some clues . . . " Lazzard looked through the notes on his map.

"I do not recommend disturbing the forest either," Dunn told Trujo. "This is a mystical place."

"I've never heard any stories like that about these woods. Only that they're massive," Renna said, watching Sallindar crouch to examine the briars in between the trees. The Tillen slipped through them suddenly, thorny underbrush rustling.

"Yes, well, your lack of knowledge is characteristic and unsurprising," Virallon said mildly.

Renna glared at him, heat flaring up her cheeks. "So is your arrogance!" she spat.

Trujo cracked a grin and Virallon bristled.

"Will you be quiet, so I can find this passage?" Lazzard waved an impatient arm at them.

"I found it." Sallindar reappeared like a specter at the edge of the woods. The others stared.

"You did not," Virallon said, astonished.

"Of course he did," Lazzard grumbled. "The Tillen live in woodlands, don't they?"

Renna slid down off Stalwart and led the nervous horse toward Sallindar. He raised an arm and held back a heavy mass of thorned bush, revealing a scarcely preserved trail. When the bush was left untouched, it created a kind of optical illusion, rendering the path invisible.

She smiled shyly at him, trying not to balk at his gaze. "Well done. Have you used it before?"

He shook his head with a slight smile, saying, "I could see it."

"I knew we brought him along for something," Trujo said and then guffawed, startling more birds overhead.

"Will you be quiet, Ralgir?" Virallon groaned as he dismounted. "There's no need to disturb the entire forest."

They pushed through the rough undergrowth, the horses nickering, until they broke free onto the trail. Then they remounted. Renna's pulse quickened as she peered into the forest gloom around them, Virallon's warnings heavy in her stomach. She plucked thorns from Stalwart's thick gray mane, murmuring soothingly to herself as well as him.

No one spoke as they rode carefully along the passage, but the melancholy chorus of insects and birds crept ever closer. Renna jumped as a random burst of trampled leaves interrupted the steady singsong. Then a swarm of strange flying worms slithered through the air, and she batted them away from her face in disgust.

The others were subdued and watchful. Dunn's head was tilted as if he were lost in thought. Sallindar's pale skin had taken on a greenish tint from the foliage around them. He alone seemed unbothered by the mysterious atmosphere. His face was relaxed, even peaceful. Perhaps it reminded him of home.

After pressing on for an hour or so, Trujo suddenly drew in a deep breath.

"Ohhh!" he sang out. "The men fought hard 'gainst the Alabass walls, but none could overturn them—"

"Be silent!" Virallon whisper-shouted. "Have you gone mad?"

"It's too quiet in here," Trujo announced, as a thousand tiny things skittered away from them through the bushes. "I like to sing when I'm traveling," he added cheerfully.

"I don't like this kind of quiet either. Better to draw out whatever's waiting," Lazzard said.

"The forest is not bothered by our presence," Sallindar said suddenly, as if he'd been listening to the trees speak. "But there are surely demons from Avid here."

"Well, the clocks were fine when the Trivineen counsel disappear—"

A sudden gasp from Dunn interrupted Virallon.

Renna wheeled about, her heart in her throat. But he was having another vision, his strange eyes unfocused and glistening.

"I see colors in the air," he murmured.

"The sky hues?" Trujo asked, confused.

"No . . . floating. Attacking from above!"

The others jerked their heads up, staring into the gloomy canopy overhead.

"When?" Lazzard drifted upward cautiously.

"What are they?" Renna asked.

Dunn shook his antlers slowly and after a moment, his beautiful eyes cleared.

"Soon. I don't know," he answered them

both. "My sight is clouded in these woods."

Virallon frowned. "I suppose we will find out soon enough. Let us make haste and watch our heads."

Chapter Five

They travelled through the forest in a jittery, paranoid state for the rest of that day, making camp only when the horses began to tire. It was a strained and uncomfortable camp. Renna rested against the side of Trujo's beast, who flopped down into the loam like a dog instead of a horse. The animal's warmth was soothing, especially in the eerie dark of the dense woods at night.

Fireflies danced in the thick blackness and Renna listened to Virallon talking softly in his sleep. Dinner had been scraped together from their supply packs, and it rolled uncomfortably in her stomach.

What would her day have been like if she were back home in Toom? She would have trained with Barrin in the morning as usual. Then walked to her mother's cottage and helped her tend the garden, so she could bring vegetables to the market. Perhaps today they would've gone to clear the weeds from her father's grave on the outskirts of the village, greeting Old Dearn there who rarely left his wife's place of rest.

Inevitably, she would've ended up sitting alone in her tiny cottage, the one Callin and others had helped her finish building shortly before the Appon's summons had arrived. The home she had hoped to share with her beloved friend.

Renna cringed backward into the sleeping animal. She hadn't allowed the thought to fully develop before, that there was so little waiting for her back home. But now it loomed over her like the black forest canopy, heavy and foreboding.

Her dream had been crushed. She would return to a lonely cottage and despair.

She decided that it was better to go on like this if she could. If she and her companions were able to resolve this crisis and reset the clocks, then she would go back to the Appon and ask if there was some further service for her. If it was her destiny to be heartbroken and alone, then she would rather keep busy doing useful work.

A soft rustle broke into her thoughts. She reached for her staff, eyes straining for movement in the dark. Then the glow of fireflies fell upon Sallindar. He was sitting up and gazing into the forest canopy. Renna looked up quickly, but all was still and black overhead. Only a faint sliver of white from the night sky hues was visible.

Whatever the night sighted Tillen could see did not worry him. He seemed lost in meditation, self-contained, and at one with the woods. Renna sighed. If only she could trade her unhappy thoughts for that kind of peace. Strange how much easier it was for her to find composure in combat.

Training to fight had first been a reaction to her father's death, encouraged by her mother for self-defense. But life in Toom was often slow and quiet, and Renna frequently found herself restless, so Umbra training had become her only release. She had hoped to find a kind of peace at Callin's side, but now . . . everything seemed empty.

*   *   *

In the morning, the travelers dragged themselves up and pushed onward, none having slept very well. Renna's back ached and her eyes were red and dry.

"I was sure I heard you snoring, Trujo, back at the Observatory Hearth," Lazzard said as they rode along. "But you've been miraculously quiet ever since."

"I only snore when I'm comfortable," Trujo replied with a cavernous yawn.

"I suppose I won't hear it again then," the Krimmer said and stretched stiffly.

"Certainly not much of a loss," Renna said.

"Indeed," Virallon chimed in and Trujo snorted.

"So says the one who talks in his sleep!"

The Scrall's wooly eyebrows shot upward. "I do not," he spluttered.

"You do," Dunn spoke up. "You speak the words of some partial spell."

Virallon gaped at them.

"Never have I heard this before," he said, grasping his beard. "What do I say? Can you repeat it?"

"Ellarune something," Renna offered.

"Idd ballid?" Dunn added. "That is all I can distinguish."

The Scrall went quiet, his yellow eyes

bright. Renna watched him curiously, but Lazzard smirked and winked at Trujo.

"Poor Vira has never had a bedfellow to tell him such things!" he declared.

Virallon turned a bright tomato-red of indignation. Renna cringed in sympathy despite the many insults she'd received from him.

"We are now much louder than when Trujo was singing," Sallindar warned.

A flash of red caught Renna's eye as Lazzard replied, "Oh, I thought the forest didn't mind?"

She looked up, thinking it must be a brilliant bird, but it was a floating circle of color. The red was quickly joined by blue and green. The three diaphanous discs hovered above their heads, descending slowly.

"The colors!" Dunn roared. "Beware!"

"What are they?" Renna gasped as the discs swept lower.

"Enemies!" Trujo declared, drawing his axe.

Renna jumped off Stalwart and yanked up her hood, summoning the Umbra state as swiftly as she could. But just as she faded into shadow, the discs suddenly disappeared.

In their place hovered thin, ragged beings with swords drawn. At first glance, they looked like Tillen children with long pale hair and bare feet. But each was the color of the disc they'd replaced—skin, hair, and clothes all saturated in red, green or blue.

In a flash, they swooped downward and struck at her visible companions. Trujo dodged as the blue one sliced at his face. Then he smashed the thing's head with his axe.

The three beings instantly vanished—and suddenly everything turned blue. Renna yelped in surprise as a panel of opaque, brilliant blue stretched across the air where they'd been.

"What in Span?" Lazzard exclaimed.

All three creatures reappeared mid-air, the blue one unscathed despite Trujo's death blow. They attacked again, slashing downward.

"Indioc! They're Indioc!" Virallon shouted as Renna blocked him from a blow. The red swordsman leapt back, startled, barely able to see her.

"Never heard of 'em," Trujo grunted, swinging at the green one.

The Scrall muttered and gestured at the strange aggressors. A bolt of hot energy narrowly missed the blue one.

Sallindar somersaulted away from the green one and Dunn fired an arrow at it. It dodged and slashed at Lazzard who slipped away. Then Renna clubbed the red one across its skull.

As one, they disappeared again. A blinding flash of red filled the air in their place.

"They do that every time you strike them?" she asked.

"Then they cannot be killed!" Dunn said in disbelief.

"There is a way!" Virallon shouted. "I must think!"

The Indioc snapped back into view, uninjured. Then the green one stabbed Lazzard deep in the shoulder. He cried out and reeled backward. Sallindar jumped up and cut the thing's throat. The air turned green as he landed on his feet, Lazzard cursing and covering his wound.

"Shields!" Dunn called out. He pulled up an iron one strapped to his horse. Sallindar and Trujo produced their own, different in shape and size.

"Quick, Scrall!" Trujo bellowed. "How do we kill the damn things?"

Renna struggled to maintain her focus. Umbra Fighting was much more effective in sustained combat than a battle that stopped and started.

The Indioc materialized and the red one saw her clearly—a sword swipe at her throat barely missed.

Fear spiked in her blood. There was no way of knowing where the fierce things would reappear, each time they were struck and vanished.

"Don't attack them!" Sallindar shouted, as if he'd read her mind. "It gives them the advantage!"

Virallon was muttering to himself and pulling on his beard, one hand forming and reforming symbols.

"Don't attack them, he says," Trujo grumbled. But he waved his weapon in front of himself defensively as two of them came at him together.

"I've got it! I remember!" Virallon called. "They must all three be killed at once!"

Dunn shot Green at that moment and the Indioc planed out into a bright green swath. The Heuwit turned swiftly to the rest of them.

"We must plan our attack and strike as one," he said, out of breath.

But when would they have time?

Renna flinched as the demons returned, Blue just inches from her. She knocked its sword aside but did not attack. It stabbed at her blindly again and again as she spun her staff, blocking the blade.

"How do we do this? Count to three?" Lazzard's voice was pained. He was fighting with his left hand and losing ground as Red pressed him. Trujo crashed his axe down upon Red's sword. Red whipped away toward Sallindar and tried to gut him.

The Tillen evaded narrowly.

"One! Two!" Trujo counted, turning toward Green.

"I don't have a hit!" Renna protested. She was still struggling with Blue.

"Nor I!" Dunn called, pointing his bow first at Blue, then Red.

"Well, get one lined up!" the Ralgir insisted.

Virallon chanted something and his hands grew sparks. "I am ready!"

No sooner had he spoken than Red threw a dagger straight into his palm. The Scrall howled in pain. Dunn shot the creature and they disappeared again.

"Virallon!" Renna gasped.

He hissed and cursed as his pony pranced fearfully underneath him. Then he raised his small shield as the Indioc returned.

"I will live," he snarled.

"One!" Sallindar cried, drawing Blue toward him.

"Two!" Renna joined in, disarming Green.

Then Green flipped in the air and smashed the top of her head with both fists.

57

She gasped and stumbled backward, fire shooting down her neck and shoulders. The world spun in place. Blackness crept into the edges of her vision.

The others shouted and colors flashed. She heard someone start off the count again and then growl in frustration.

Stalwart was suddenly at her side, and she grasped the reins, leaning into him. The blackness was beginning to fade, but not the pain. She squinted through it at the ongoing battle.

Even when the Indioc were disarmed before being hit, they reappeared with new swords in hand. How was it possible? Where did they go when they vanished? They seemed indestructible, whipping in and out, stabbing and slicing.

Sallindar yelled, "Now!" but only swearing and grunting followed.

The forest had gone dead quiet around the struggle as if waiting to see who would win.

Lazzard's shoulder was bleeding as he fought awkwardly with his other arm. Virallon struggled to conjure energy, but he turned pale and huddled over his injured hand.

"One!" Dunn called out.

"Wait!" Lazzard stabbed Green just in time before it gutted him.

Renna tried to clear her head as the air turned green. She ducked right afterward, knowing the Indioc would be back in moments. She blinked and looked up when the fighting sprang up again. The best way she could help now was to help line up the attack, but her vision blurred as she tried to keep track of her companions.

"One!" Lazzard shouted, then, "Ugh, nevermind," just as Sallinder added, "Two!"

"Curse these miserable little—" Trujo's words ended in a growl.

Dunn gored Red in frustration and the space above them flared crimson. Renna's eyes finally cleared as the Indioc returned. She saw Trujo hook his great arm around Blue's head and hold tight, looking to the others. Sallindar kicked Green's sword away from him.

She looked at Dunn: The Heuwit yanked one of his arrows away from Red, who had grabbed hold of it after losing its blade. Dunn raised the arrow like a dagger at the same time Sallindar lunged for Green.

Her heart leapt as she realized they each had a chance.

"Now!" she shouted. The effort throbbed horribly in her head.

Trujo snapped Blue's neck; Sallindar pierced Green in the heart; Dunn stabbed Red with his arrow.

Then suddenly the air turned into a sea of color. Not like the sky hues, but a violent mesh of green, blue, and red. Renna braced herself, staring into the wash, afraid of what might spring out next.

But nothing did. Slowly, the colors dissolved into nothing. No Indioc reappeared.

A bird or squirrel chirruped somewhere nearby, breaking the watchful silence.

A heartbeat later, Lazzard sank to the ground.

Sallindar rushed to the pack on his horse and pulled out a small packet of herbs. Dunn unrolled a bandage from his own supplies, then they surrounded the wilted Krimmer.

"I'm a champion. I won't be felled by a shoulder wound," he argued as Trujo held him up.

Virallon hissed at his own injury. Renna took hold of Stalwart's reins and stumbled toward him, leaning on the horse's side. The Scrall's punctured hand was so small, it made the dagger look like a sword.

"It'll hurt like death when we pull it out," she said with sympathy.

"I'll have no one else but Sallindar," he grumbled. "The rest of you would make a mess of it."

Chapter Six

Elix sat cross-legged on the floor of the clock chamber, aware that if Anderin were to see him in such a pose, he would be appalled. He was not standing alert and focused, secure in the recognition of the importance of his role.

But Anderin would never enter the chamber out of turn, so it did not matter. Elix sat like a dejected child, listening to the whispers of the shapeshifter who called himself Skink . . . who slid around columns and lurked in the corners, his eyes gleaming in his pointed blue face . . . murmuring promises, wheedling, cooing.

"Have you ever felt the sky colors glow on your face, Clock Keeper? So warm and magnificent."

"Have you not dreamed of standing in the wind?"

Elix lowered his head, unable to bear the longing. The sensation had first surfaced years ago. He was not supposed to even consider such things. Something had gone wrong when the Appon had made him; that was apparent when he compared himself to Anderin, who seemed mindlessly content.

But the anomaly was not his fault. How could it be? And why should he suffer for it?

"I could give you a way out of this prison, Clock Keeper."

Elix dared not move, his contracted heart working itself harder. The sluggish blood in his veins surged and he flinched involuntarily. Skink caught the movement like a spider snagging a fly.

"I know an old spell," he whispered, "That would make a hole in the seal on the tower."

A thousand warnings fired off in Elix's mind. Yet none of them seemed as important at that moment as leaving the dark tower and basking in the sky hues.

What this monster meant to do to Span, however, would *destroy* it. How much time would he actually have out there in the beautiful outdoors?

Elix shivered and glared at Skink with his blank white eyes. But the shapeshifter was shrewd, anticipating his thoughts.

"Freedom in a dark world is better than none at all," he said. "Is it not so?"

*   *   *

It was a sight for everyone's sore eyes two days later, when the trees of the dark Aggard gave way to a lush, open meadow. Lazzard and Virallon were bandaged and healing, but no one was rested. Each night, even when it wasn't her turn to keep watch, Renna found herself clutching her staff and staring out into the dark, waiting for another attack. The way the others stumbled around in the morning suggested that they did the same.

Virallon had taken to speaking softly to himself, occasionally twirling his uninjured hand this way and then the other. Renna caught a few of the words that he spoke in his sleep. She wondered what he was attempting.

"What are the Indioc?" she had asked him, after the dagger had been withdrawn and his hand was wrapped up tight.

"Even you humans must know of the Swirls, the source of the sky hues and all other colors," Virallon said with a grimace of pain. "They were here long before the Appon arrived. But I suppose it would be a surprise if you knew of the legends of their protectors. The Indioc are guardians born directly of the Swirl waters. Sprites, of a sort."

"There is a large Swirl outside of Mustin, but I have not heard of one near here," Dunn said. "Why would they consider us a threat?"

"They attacked us out of the blue!" Trujo added.

"And the red and the green," Lazzard muttered.

"The ancient guardians I speak of are known as the Indioc, but those demons that attacked us are some twisted version, with no real purpose here," Virallon told them. "I recall reading that some of them went astray when Lugis synced the clocks."

"So you might have been wrong about how to kill them," Lazzard said, wincing as he mounted his horse.

"But I wasn't," Virallon snapped.

Renna glanced at Sallindar and saw that he was studying her, perhaps because of her own

63

injury. She was still clinging to Stalwart and her neck ached when she tried to turn her head. She would not have the same range of motion for a little while.

"I thought the Swirls were legends," she told him quietly.

He shook his head.

"Have you seen one?" she asked.

"I have." He mounted his white horse and asked, "Can you ride?"

Renna's mind drifted a moment as she imagined gazing at something as luminous and uncanny as a lagoon of rainbow-hued water. A well-spring from which every visible coloration in the world emerged, from the dancing chroma of the sky to the tiniest petals, scales, and fibers.

Her grandfather had described the Swirls to her when she was very young, but her practical-minded father had scoffed at the story. They were a myth, he'd said, disappointing Renna. She heard various tales about them later, but never any first-hand accounts. Few people in her village had traveled much out in the world.

"I want to see one someday." She climbed up onto Stalwart's back, adding, "Some people say they grant immortality."

Lazzard scoffed at that. "Humans claim immortality as a side effect of most natural phenomena, don't they? Any hidden spring of water, or odd-looking crystal."

Renna scowled. "We do *not.*"

Her neck was still stiff when they reached the welcome meadow, its glory taking them all by surprise. The trees had been thinning and the daylight growing stronger, but no one had expected such a brilliant field of flowers and open sky. Not in the midst of such a dark wood.

"Is it a mirage?" Lazzard asked, squinting in the sun.

"It's the heart of the Aggard," Virallon said warily. "Let us hasten through it."

He gave no explanation for his unease, but the others took his cue and rode quietly into the sea of blue and purple petals. Renna's muscles slackened in the warmth of the sky, and she sighed, breathing in the sweet perfume of the flowers.

A golden haze hung low over the meadow and tiny, flitting beings—all geometric eyes, fur, and colored wings—buzzed in the air, lulling her into a kind of daydream. They were much more pleasant than the flying worms.

Trujo cracked a gigantic yawn nearby. "This makes me long for a warm bed."

"This makes me long for a warm bed and a woman," Lazzard replied, winking at Renna. She ignored him. "How about you, Sallindar? What do you long for?" he asked mockingly.

The Tillen said nothing for a moment, watching a winged being flash by him.

"I long to know whether I'm truly this drowsy or if it's the work of some magic."

Renna stifled a yawn, alarmed.

"I was wondering the same thing myself," Virallon said in a sleepy voice.

Trujo groaned. "Can't it just be a nice meadow?"

"If it's magic, who's casting it?" Renna asked. The meadow was quiet apart from the stirring of the grasses and flowers.

"Not these little spitting things." Lazzard swatted at one of them half-heartedly.

"No indeed. Something powerful," Virallon said, frowning. "I suspected that the heart of the forest would contain a potent force of some kind."

"Perhaps it's unintentional," Sallindar told him.

"How could anyone accidentally make us sleepy?" Lazzard asked with a sneer.

"Some creatures' methods of defense affect everyone differently," Sallindar said in his light rasp. "Like the Tralling."

"True," Virallon said, raising an impressed eyebrow. "The Tralling confuse the senses when they release their defensive signals. They cause some to hear wailing noises and others to see flashes of light, and so on."

The Tralling were rarely seen creatures that possessed many webbed digits and gleaming eyes, and lurked in the muddy layers of wetlands. Renna had heard that they often caused travelers to lose their way and turn back, which had led to some wetlands being deemed haunted or cursed before the discovery of the low-lying creatures.

"Have you experienced this?" Dunn asked Sallindar.

He nodded. "I was very young, but it made an impression. I could still send the memory."

Renna looked back at him as Trujo yawned again.

"Can you send memories?" she asked, intrigued.

He nodded again.

66

"I have read that the Tillen are emotionally bound to each other, capable of sharing their thoughts and emotions," Virallon said as a breeze swept the tall grasses around them. "Even experiencing each other's pain."

"That sounds uncomfortable," Trujo commented.

Renna noticed that Dunn had gone still, a familiar sheen over his eyes.

"It's only between loved ones, in close proximity," Sallindar explained.

"So if I were to strike you down, Sallindar, I'd be taking out any nearby kinfolk as well?" Lazzard asked, amused.

Renna opened her mouth to draw their attention to Dunn, but Sallindar smiled defiantly, surprising her. It was the most animated expression he'd made yet.

"You'd be lucky to get as far as the first part," he said.

"Oh, ho!" Trujo barked a great laugh.

Lazzard reddened, his anger rising.

"Dunn?" Renna asked quickly, distracting them.

They all looked at the Heuwit.

"Something has . . . gone terribly wrong," he whispered, reining in his horse. "The worst is about to happen."

As he spoke, the flowers and grasses suddenly rustled faster, sending their winged friends scurrying away toward the trees.

"Right now?" Renna asked, eyes wide.

She couldn't see anything, but something was clearly in the meadow with them, whether or not it was related. Stalwart stopped walking of his own accord, and nervously turned his head side to side.

Sallindar, Lazzard, and Trujo drew their weapons, slowing their horses and staring across the rippling field. Renna dismounted and pulled up her hood. Then she realized that Dunn was still in his trance. She stepped swiftly toward the Heuwit just as Sallindar rode up to guard him too.

There was time left for a single breath.

Then a swarm of small creatures rushed out at them. They burst from the tall grass with claws and fangs flashing: hairless, muscular demons with leathery blue skin.

Renna slipped into her Umbra state and whirled into them, spinning her staff. But the drowsiness clung to her and slowed her reflexes. Despite her near invisibility, she almost caught a slash in her stomach.

Virallon shot electric bolts into the hoard while Lazzard swooped down into them, stabbing blue throats and bellies. But both were struggling to keep their eyes open. Even Sallindar, fighting from his horse in front of Dunn, kept shaking his head clear.

"Blasted little . . . pests," Trujo grumbled, swinging his axe.

In the back of her blurred mind, Renna recognized their assailants as Rungers. She'd seen drawings of them in old stories, acting as henchmen of Lugis and larger Avidian beasts. They were small but relentless, plowing through the field as if they were driven by something behind them. The ground shook with the force of the onslaught.

"We could use you, Heuwit!" Lazzard yelled, kicking two of them off his legs. "Wake up and fight!"

Dunn blinked and then snapped back to the present with a fierce shake of his antlers. That left Sallindar free to spring from his horse and slice apart several Rungers. Inky blood flew into the air, swiftly followed by arrows from Dunn.

Renna stumbled, blinking, and a Runger swiped its claws through her cloak. She smacked it sideways with her staff, trying to focus. The warm, soft ground was calling to her. She wanted desperately to lay down.

"Where are these demons coming from?" Lazzard demanded. "Are they sprouting from the dirt?"

Virallon had no answer. He was busy charring as many as he could with his spells, his bandaged hand trembling with the effort.

Renna's focus collapsed as the sleepiness overwhelmed her. She was suddenly in clear view, and the Rungers threw themselves upon her. They bit and tore at her arms. With a frustrated grunt, she twisted away and swept her staff across a line of their heads.

Sallindar threw several of the Rungers bodily and Trujo began doing the same, flinging them off his axe back into the tall grasses.

"This was not my vision!" Dunn informed them as he speared two Rungers on his antlers.

"And these aren't the cause of our lethargy!" Virallon smacked a jumping Runger with his shield, then scorched two others. "These are minions!"

"I can't even fight minions if I'm falling

asleep!" Trujo roared. He swung his axe wildly, nearly catching Virallon in the head.

"Careful, you fool—" the Scrall's shout warped into a yawn.

Renna lost her focus again, eyelids drooping. Three Rungers leapt upon her at once and she staggered. But one of them slumped and dropped to the ground, unexpectedly.

The other two caught hold of Renna's staff and hung on as she swung it. But one suddenly closed its eyes and fell. The next to come charging behind it stumbled and fell also—yawning.

"They are . . . tiring also," Dunn gasped, letting loose an arrow that went wide.

Renna glanced up at the oncoming stream. The Rungers were still pouring out from the grass, but now they were drooping afterward, tripping over each other and collapsing.

"Thank the blasted sky hues," Lazzard cursed, hovering above them. He was pressing a hand against his bound shoulder wound.

Sallindar held out his arms, signaling the rest of them to hold back. The Rungers that plunged forward were now falling on top of each other, piling up dark blue bodies.

Renna heaved a sigh and leaned against Stalwart, whose breathing suggested he was half-asleep. She forced her eyes open and saw Lazzard land sloppily back into his saddle.

"Let's go," Trujo said sleepily.

"Yes, now," Virallon said and clumsily gathered his reins.

Renna mounted Stalwart as fast as she could. The poor horse snorted awake and stumbled forward. The group of them tripped and pitched their way across the meadow, headed for the shadows of the woods on the other side.

She looked back once and saw the stream of Rungers finally dwindling to a halt. There was a small hill of them dozing in the grass now, almost like the Spinners back in Gwin.

Deep within the trees, the travelers stopped to get their bearings. Everyone stepped back from Dunn as he shook his antlers in a wide arc to wake himself up. With the return of the chill and gloom, their sleepiness abruptly faded.

Amazed, Renna felt her senses sharpen once again.

"It's the meadow itself that causes fatigue," Sallindar said, wiping his sword clean. They were all dripping with the Rungers' indigo blood.

"How?" Renna asked just as Lazzard demanded, "Why?"

"The heart of the Aggard must protect itself," Virallon replied, wincing at the pain in his hand.

"Protect itself from what?" Trujo asked.

Looking at the rest of them, Renna suddenly thought she understood. Altogether they were quite intimidating.

"From violence," she said. "We're carrying weapons, so we look like a threat. And the Rungers were obviously on the attack . . . So it tried to put us all to sleep."

"Couldn't they see our Appon badges?" Lazzard asked snarkily.

Renna looked up as the forest creaked and rustled overhead, the sky already vanished behind the thick canopy. She was impressed by the defensive trick, but it chilled her a moment. What would have happened if they hadn't escaped the meadow? Would they had slept forever?

Chapter Seven

They rode a rough, tangled path through the forest until darkness fell. Then they made camp in a cold, damp hollow. Sinking to the ground with a shiver, Renna thought ruefully of the sunny warmth in the meadow they'd left behind.

Her cloak had hung unusually limp since the Runger attack and now she examined the jagged holes in the thick cloth. They would affect her Umbra Combat ability if not repaired, so she pulled her needle and thread from her pack as Dunn took off to hunt.

"Ralgir wounds don't take so long to heal," Trujo told Lazzard. The Krimmer was standing motionless, white-faced and strained, as blood seeped through the dressing on his shoulder.

Virallon appeared to be dozing off already, clutching his injured hand.

"Neither do Krimmer's if we don't keep aggravating them," Lazzard replied.

Sallindar studied him a moment and then went to his horse.

"Does it need sewing up?" Renna asked, holding up her kit.

Lazzard gaped at her in horror. "Sewing up? What human madness is this?"

She snorted. Trujo appeared similarly shocked.

"It isn't nice to look at, but it does work," she said. "You have to make do however you can if you don't have magic." She raised her eyebrows at him, grinning. "Haven't you learned anything from your 'several affairs?'"

"I don't know what *you* call affairs, but I was sleeping with those humans, Renna, not fighting them."

Lazzard looked sharply at Sallindar as the Tillen approached him, unwinding a yellow cloth in his hands.

"And what Tillen madness is this?" he asked.

"This is from the Kubula plant," Sallindar said. "It will hold the wound closed better than your bandage."

Grudgingly, Lazzard undid his stained shirt and began to peel off his soaked wrapping. The herbs underneath fell to the ground in a soggy mess and Renna had to look away, her stomach lurching. She was grateful she would not have to stitch him up.

"You must remove your shirt," Sallindar told him.

"Why?" Lazzard asked.

The Tillen gestured that he needed to wrap the cloth under Lazzard's arm and over the shoulder.

"You can tuck it under the shirt," the Krimmer said, frowning, but Sallindar shook his

74

head. "Are you so anxious to see me unclothed, Tillen?"

"What's the problem, Lazzard?" Trujo asked with a grin. "Embarrassed by your lack of muscle?"

Renna looked up, wondering why Lazzard was so reluctant. It would have been more like him to call attention to the fact that he was undressing and make a joke about it. But his mouth was set into a hard line.

"Maybe I don't want to put you to shame, Trujo," he said.

Sallindar shrugged, turning away. "It won't work unless the whole cloth touches the skin."

"Don't be a fool," Renna told Lazzard. "Your wound is not healing."

Virallon woke up in time to hear her and rubbed the web of wrinkles around his eyes, looking at the scowling Krimmer.

"Your concern for my recovery is touching," Lazzard snapped. He yanked off his shirt roughly and then gasped in pain.

Renna's sympathies stirred at the idea that he might be self-conscious about his body. That was something she could certainly identify with, especially as a woman who had trained in combat with mostly men. She had often been grateful for her slight figure, assuming it was less distracting. That wasn't always the case though.

As Sallindar approached Lazzard with caution, she got up to help, saying, "There's no need to worry about judgement from us—"

"Spare me your speech," he spat.

Taken back, she fell silent. She stepped behind him to pass the Kubula cloth over his bare shoulder back to Sallindar. Then she saw the bumps.

There were two of them between Lazzard's shoulder blades, each the size of an orange. He circled nervously, trying to hide them, but Sallindar moved with him, pressing the cloth ends together.

The Tillen caught sight of the bumps and hesitated for a fraction of an instant.

Renna saw Virallon's eyes fall upon them and then narrow. It obviously meant something significant to him. To her, they resembled the nubs left by limbs that had been removed. But what limbs would Lazzard have had on his back?

On anyone else, she would have guessed they were wings. But Krimmers flew without them.

The pale cloth clung instantly to Lazzard's skin as if it were alive. He flinched instinctively and then relaxed, studying it. Then he snatched up his shirt and carefully pulled it back on.

Virallon was eyeing him with a suspicious frown.

"The wrap holds by itself?" Renna asked Sallindar, amazed.

He nodded, heading back to his pack.

"My kind have cultivated the Kubula for so long that we can communicate with it, and it's usually cooperative."

"The Appon first developed the Kubula plant," Virallon told them all. "But it's extremely difficult to grow—"

"Fascinating," Lazzard said shortly. He rotated his arm, wincing, and the yellow wrap held firm. Sallindar brought Virallon another Kubula bandage for his hand.

"Don't be so impatient with the knowledge of your elders, Krimmer," the Scrall grumbled.

"When I have asked for it, I am always patient to hear it," came the retort.

Renna watched the Tillen bind Virallon's hand. Her neck still ached and was frustratingly stiff, but she had no serious open wounds.

"Do those work on Umbra cloaks?" she asked with a smile.

He shook his head and smiled back—not the fierce grin he'd given Lazzard before. But something light and sweet, that softened his stony face.

Renna's pulse quickened, surprising her. She dropped her eyes to the deep black cloth in her lap. It stirred slightly in response to her emotion, and she pushed her needle through to quell it.

She thought about how it had stirred whenever she'd worn it near Callin. Then she bit her lip. This was the last thing she had expected, to be attracted to one of her companions! Especially not while her heart was still healing. . . Especially *not* to the inscrutable Tillen. Surely he was not even interested in humans.

It was foolish, either way, considering their situation. So, she did her best to ignore it.

When Dunn returned a few moments later with greens and fresh meat, it brightened everyone's mood. Trujo built a fire, and they gathered around it to eat, listening to the eerie crackings and rustlings of the Aggard Forest.

The horses grazed quietly nearby, their ears twitching at each sound.

"Heuwit, I'd almost forgotten. What was

your vision in the meadow?" Virallon asked.

Dunn chewed his leaves, staring into the fire.

"I saw a darkened sky." His rich voice drifted over them in a kind of singsong warning. Renna watched him, worried.

"And an army of motley creatures," he said as the embers swirled around the fire. "Raising their heads up . . . to howl in demonic joy."

*   *   *

"Smoke," Sallindar said, lifting his nose toward the wind.

"Ashes," Dunn agreed, giving a loud sniff.

They were approaching the end of the woods, according to Lazzard's maps, but the trees were still thick and close as ever. The only sign was the thinning of the undergrowth.

"Campfire?" Renna asked, wary of whom they might disturb.

"No," Sallindar said, and his tone worried her even more.

"I don't smell anything," Trujo declared.

"Nor do I," Virallon said. "But I trust your noses. Is it a forest fire?"

"We are too far away to tell," Dunn replied and urged his horse to go faster. The others picked up the speed as well.

"Is it wise to rush directly into it?" Lazzard grumbled, snagging his sleeve on a branch. He had been noticeably sullener since Sallindar wrapped his shoulder wound.

"Not feeling like a champion today, eh?"

Trujo called back to him.

Virallon harrumphed with a satisfaction that rankled the Krimmer. He flew up off his horse, scratching himself on more branches.

"Or perhaps I'm the only champion here with any sense!" he declared. "I'll go up and see where the holocaust is, shall I?"

Then he disappeared among the treetops. It was so sudden that it took Renna a moment to notice his horse was left behind. She turned back and caught the poor thing's reins, leading him along. He and Stalwart touched noses as if in mutual exasperation at their riders.

It wasn't long before the sharp tang of smoke hit her nose and throat. The Krimmer still hadn't returned when the forest suddenly ended, tumbling out into a stretch of open fields . . . under an oddly dim sky.

A haze of black smoke hovered over the town that lay directly ahead.

"Reegins Stone!" Virallon exclaimed. "Is it under attack?"

As they watched, part of the blackened town wall crumbled, ashes swirling.

"Where's Lazzard?" Trujo asked, looking up.

Renna followed suit and frowned at the muted sky. There were few clouds, but the color patterns were dull and lackluster. She had expected to be blinded by them after their many days in the dense woods.

"The darkened sky," Dunn murmured, alarmed.

Everyone drew their weapons, tension

mounting.

"Where *is* Lazzard?" Virallon asked, looking first upward and then back into the forest.

"He will find us," Dunn said quickly. "Let us make for the town."

They rode out under the strange sky, and the wind that whipped against them made the smoke dance wickedly above the town of Reegins Stone.

No one spoke as they passed through the abandoned gate, choking and coughing in the snowfall of ashes. A litany of charred objects lay in the streets. Some were clearly bodies and Renna looked quickly away. An outstretched arm made her stomach lurch.

The building roofs were sunken in and gutted, with their beams jutting out like ribcages.

"I was here only a few months ago," Dunn said in disbelief.

"This could be the work of a Zin," Virallon said quietly. "The Appon has received reports of them since the clocks were altered."

"The Living Fires?" Dunn asked, alarmed.

It was yet another race that Renna only vaguely knew, one not seen since the days of Lugis and Santir. The Zins were beings of pure flame that swept through cities and towns at terrifying speeds.

Something crackled and Renna flinched, gripping her staff. A long strip of cloth lay burning on the ground nearby. The group of them watched it for a moment in silence.

Renna wondered numbly how many lives had been lost.

Trujo swung down from his mount and snorted in disgust. He stomped on the small fire, putting it out.

A second later, he roared and leapt away—as a geyser of flames burst up from the spot.

The horses screamed and reared in terror. Renna clung to Stalwart as the fire stream shot into the sky. He wheeled and bolted for the gate, along with Virallon's pony and Lazzard's horse. She reined him in desperately as the other animals tried to escape in different directions.

At that moment, Lazzard swept down from the sky, his eyes wide at the flames. He caught his horse's reins and sank back onto the saddle.

Over her shoulder, Renna saw the column of fire shrink and morph into something like a figure. Heat enveloped her as if she stood by an open oven. The fiery figure crackled in place, moving its pseudo-limbs slowly like a newborn testing them out.

"By Alabass!" Trujo breathed.

The Zin fixed them with a terrifying stare made of vague facial features. Sweat trickled down Renna's face and neck as Stalwart whinnied and backed away again. She longed to flee just as much as he did.

"Are you the one responsible for this destruction?" Virallon demanded, barely restraining his pony.

The creature of fire twirled in place and gave them something like a smile. Then several small flames broke out at once among the rubble around them.

"It would seem he's not alone!" Lazzard called out.

Renna's gut clenched and her sweat froze in

cold fear. They could be engulfed in flames in a matter of seconds.

Then Virallon suddenly shouted, "Ellarune . . . idd . . . *ballidare!*"

The air shimmered spectacularly over his head. Renna looked up and saw a glassy film hovering, sliding down around them. Her heart leapt.

A shield? Had he cast a protective shield?

The pulsing layer suddenly convulsed and then disappeared. Virallon cursed as more flames burst to life all around them.

"The cistern!" Dunn hollered. "Run!"

The Heuwit's giant horse did not hesitate. He raced forward and to the right—just as swirling balls of fire streaked toward them.

Renna screamed, ducking and clinging to Stalwart as he raced after Dunn. In an instant, her clothes were drenched with sweat. The overpowering heat stole her breath. Smoke stung her eyes and filled her throat. The flying wheels of flame shot past her left and right as Stalwart's hooves pounded the cobblestones.

"This way!" Dunn's voice rang out.

She could not see him in the nightmare air, but she followed the sound, choking and crying burning tears. The rider's horse nearest her suddenly let loose an awful scream. She spun Stalwart around as hot blasts whizzed past them.

It was Sallindar—she could just make him out as he dumped his water pouch onto his terrified, burning horse.

"Go on!" he shouted, struggling to stay in the saddle.

She tossed him her own water pouch, then let Stalwart streak away. In another moment, she had burst through a mass of smoke to see Virallon and Dunn, their horses huddled near an enormous, enclosed well. Despite her streaming eyes, she saw that the air around them was clearer.

The Zins had left a berth between themselves and the cistern.

Trujo and Lazzard raced past her an instant later.

"Your cloak!" Trujo rasped over his shoulder.

Renna rode up to the edge of the cistern and slid frantically off her horse. One corner of her cloak was on fire and the whole thing was shuddering. She tore it off her and stamped on the flames, deep coughs wracking her throat.

Sallindar clattered into the ring of safety a few seconds later. He jumped off his crying horse and poured more water on its wounded side.

Everyone's faces were ashy, their eyes red.

A line of Zins gathered about ten feet away from them, advancing and withdrawing in a rhythmic, menacing pattern.

Renna gasped at the sight and backed up against the cowering Stalwart.

She tried to ask, "Can we open the well?" but her voice was nothing but a hoarse whisper.

"Why don't they throw fire at us?" Lazzard asked in a husky voice.

"They are connected, like my people," Sallindar said, staring at them. "If you douse one flame, they all feel it."

Virallon cried out before anyone else could

speak. His robe had been smoldering, unnoticed, and suddenly burst into flame. Trujo snatched him up like a child and began beating out the fire.

Renna's head spun as she watched them. She had inhaled too much smoke. She sank to the ground in her soaked clothes and struggled to breathe.

The fire demons had them surrounded, crackling and waiting. Her vision swam, and blackness filtered in and out.

"Leave me be!" Virallon spluttered distantly. "Broken bones do not heal burns!"

Everything drifted away from Renna for a moment. She felt her head slump forward, but even that motion seemed far away.

All of a sudden, Sallindar's voice tore through the darkness.

"Hold her up," he said to someone, and then, "Drink this," to her.

She felt Trujo's tree trunk arm against her back and opened her eyes to see a drinking pouch aimed at her mouth. She drank carefully, a warm, foul herbal mixture slipping down her throat. It was so thick and strong that she wretched, spitting out ashes along with the herbs.

"Ugh!" She choked out more and shivered wretchedly.

"Are you poisoning her, Tillen?" Lazzard asked from somewhere nearby.

"Clearing her throat," Sallindar said. He was kneeling next to her, his smoke-darkened face studying her own.

She took in a large, shaky breath. She was still weak and dizzy, but she could feel her lungs refilling. It was with relief as much as air.

The others turned back to look at the wall of Zins, who were still undulating, sorely tempted to rush closer to the cistern.

"They are waiting until we venture away from the water source. Which we must do eventually," Dunn said. Even his musical voice was coated thick. "Virallon, how can we fight these creatures?"

"There is a spell to ward them off," the Scrall croaked. "I must think . . . I need a moment."

They waited pensively, coughing and rubbing their eyes. Renna longed for the water pouch she'd given to Salendar.

Then there came a loud clank and the sound of a sliding bolt. Everyone whirled at the sound except for Renna, who simply turned her weary head.

The cistern was being opened from the inside.

A hollow voice floated upward. "I know the spell."

Then a human climbed out slowly, dripping water from long, brown robes. His cloak bore the ribbon-and-pamphlet symbol of the Envoy Guild. He was middle-aged with short, dark hair that was rapidly turning white. He regarded them with solemn eyes above a broad nose.

"Friend or foe?" Trujo asked him hoarsely.

"My name is Endi," he replied, shielding his eyes and staring at the Zins. "I am a messenger."

"From an underwater world?" Lazzard asked with an eyebrow raised.

"I've been hiding in there—it's half empty. I

85

reached Reegins Stone yesterday, exhausted, and knew I'd better spend the night near a water source. The town was already ravaged."

"You're from the Envoy Guild," Renna said, coughing.

She recognized the symbol from those who had visited Toom in the past. Most of the league of messengers were human; it was an organization that her race had founded.

"Yes, but luckily, I do know some magic."

So saying, Endi squared his shoulders and stared directly at the Zins. Then he held out his arms.

"Awindos acquinus! *Acquinus!*" he shouted.

The light around them suddenly flashed. It grew so bright that Renna squeezed her eyes closed, pain stabbing her temples. When she forced them open a moment later, she caught sight of the Zins frozen in place, their "mouths" wide open.

Then they burned away to nothing, ashes dropping to the ground.

The sudden stillness was incredible. Renna got to her feet and gazed out at the smoky emptiness where the Zins had danced just moments before.

"If you can do *that*, Envoy, why in the world were you hiding?" Lazzard asked.

"The effect is temporary," Virallon said wearily. "They come back."

Endi nodded. "I used it to get myself to the cistern and then rest."

"How long do we have until they return?" Dunn asked, mounting his horse.

"Time enough if we ride fast." Endi gathered his robes in a hurry. "I see you bear the emblem of the Appon and so I give you my trust. May I share your steed?"

Dunn reached down and helped the man up behind him as Renna hurried to climb upon Stalwart. They all turned quickly toward the gates, urging the reluctant horses back into the smoke.

"Go, Stalwart! It's our only way out!" she shouted, kicking him.

Sallindar's poor injured horse stalled, shaking its head and crying. Sallindar whispered something to it, but still it balked. Then Trujo raced his animal forward and grabbed the reins from the Tillen, propelling them ahead as a unit. The white horse screamed as they stumbled back through the town, the cries slicing through Renna's heart.

Before they could reach the town wall, the Zins blazed up again with a sickening roar. Renna screamed herself, echoing the horse. The heat smothered her and she closed her eyes, clinging blindly to Stalwart as he wheeled in panic.

Virallon and Endi shouted together, "Awindos acquinus! Acquinus!"

Then the blinding light seared through her eyelids. As soon as the Zins faded, Stalwart was off again, needing no encouragement. Just before the gate, the fires flared up again. This time, Renna screamed the spell along with the others.

Only then did the nightmare end—but the horses didn't stop. They burst through the gate and kept on running. They rode as far as they could from the ruined walls of Reegins Stone, steam rising from their flanks and into the strange sky.

Chapter Eight

"It is serendipitous that I ran into you," Endi told them. His face was shaded green behind waving leaves.

He had led the way to a distant field of damp, slit-leaved plants that were soothing to the skin. The champions had nearly fallen off their exhausted mounts, sinking into the softness of the strange growth. The plants were cool and moist, and smelled of strong herbs.

Renna gingerly rolled up her sleeves and pants to place the leaves against her singed skin. She sucked in her breath as the plants burned for just an instant before they turned cold.

Trujo lay flat on his back, crushing a wide expanse, while the others tended to their own burns.

Around them were small groves of trees and a winding ribbon creek that vanished into the tall grass. It was a blissful retreat.

Sallindar spoke softly to his pale horse and persuaded it to kneel, snorting and cringing, into the healing plants. Renna brought a few handfuls of the leaves up to Stalwart and rubbed his sides. He pressed his nose into her shoulder.

"Do you have more of your Kubula wraps?" she asked Sallindar.

"No," he said, stroking the horse's white mane. "But this elderline will ease his suffering." He began gathering the leaves to stuff into his pack.

"I never knew such plants existed," Dunn said, his deep voice weary.

"It was a Tillen who first showed me this place," Endi said with a nod. "Elderline is beneficial in many ways. Some humans even believe that eating them can grant immortality."

Lazzard barked a laugh and cast a side glance at Renna. She frowned.

"How did you know of the spell to extinguish Zins?" Virallon asked Endi, with a hint of disapproval.

"As a youth, I studied at the Scralls' great library in West Iddiren," the messenger told him. "But I was forbidden to continue past a certain level, since I'm a human."

Renna glared at Virallon, but the Scrall nodded as if that were only just.

"May I ask what message you're carrying?" he asked, his brows knitted together.

Endi met the Scrall's yellow gaze in silence for a moment.

"I imagine that's private," Lazzard told Virallon.

"In fact, it is not," the Envoy said quietly. "It is for everyone that I encounter, and it is terrible news indeed." He sighed. "The unthinkable has happened."

"No," Virallon murmured. "The clocks!"

Renna froze, looking from one to the other.

"Yes," Endi said sadly. "They have been synced."

Her stomach turned a sickening loop. As the others stared at the Envoy, stunned into silence, she sank slowly backward into the damp plants.

Was it over then? Had they failed already?

The muted sky floated above her, framed by elderline stems, and her sore skin rubbed against her filthy clothes. It was early afternoon, but somehow it looked like twilight.

Then it suddenly dawned on her why.

"It is . . . what I saw in my vision," Dunn said solemnly. "I did not want to believe it."

"How did this happen?" Lazzard demanded. "I thought the Clock Keepers killed that shapeshifter!"

"So we were told," Endi told him. "But the Appon knew at once when the sky darkened, and then the news of devastating attacks immediately poured in. They summoned my guild to spread the warning."

"Did the shapeshifter have a partner?" Trujo asked, incredulous, as Renna sat back up.

Her companions' faces were stony, but she felt tears fluttering under her eyelids. Surely champions did not cry. She wiped a fist across her face and stared at the damp ground.

Endi looked at Virallon again as he answered Trujo. "The Appon suspect that we have been betrayed . . . by the Clock Keepers themselves."

"No!" This time, Virallon hissed like a cat. He glared across the field in the direction of the Time Tower.

"Why do they suspect this?" Dunn asked Endi.

"Because everyone suspects betrayal, from all sides," Lazzard said with surprising bitterness.

Virallon glanced at him shrewdly.

"It is because the Clock Keepers sealed themselves inside the tower after the first incident," Endi explained. "And no one has been able to go in or out. So if the shapeshifter was truly destroyed, then only the Clock Keepers could be at fault."

"But how could a being who was only created for one purpose turn around and betray that purpose?" Dunn asked.

"Perhaps he was tired of it," Sallindar said, rising to his feet.

"If that was a jest, it was in poor taste, considering the circumstances," Virallon growled.

Sallindar shook his head in mild surprise. "It wasn't."

"I used to wonder the same thing when I was back in Toom," Renna told them all. "Whether or not the Clock Keepers could really go on serving their purpose forever. But we won't understand anything until we reach the tower."

"Yes. We must go." Virallon got to his feet, stiff and sore. He paused then and squinted down at his hands. "Wait just a moment," he said, as the rest of them stood.

They watched him curiously as he closed his eyes, concentrating. A moment later, he flung up his hands, reciting the first words he'd shouted in Reegins Stone.

"Ellarune idd ballidare!"

This time, the air around them warped and

bubbled. Renna gasped as it caught the light like a prism and then billowed out beyond their seven figures in the grass. Like a dome, it sealed down over them, glistening softly.

"A shield," Endi breathed. "Well done!"

Virallon sighed and reddened with pride. He nodded briskly, as the others turned in a circle, staring in wonder at the walls of the wavering bubble.

Sallindar tilted his head in admiration; even Lazzard looked grudgingly impressed.

"I suppose my abilities have strengthened in my old age," Virallon told them. "Never could I cast one before."

The Krimmer picked up a stone and tossed it through the shield. The protection held as the rock fell to the ground on the other side.

"Is *that* what you were doing in your sleep?" Renna asked Virallon.

"I believe that my inner mind was attempting it, yes." He waved his good hand once more and the shield vanished. "It's draining to maintain it, but I should improve."

"This will certainly work to our advantage," Dunn told him, his tone more hopeful than before. Renna's spirits lifted as well.

"Yes, Vira, I'm quite taken aback. What else are you hiding in that tiny noggin?" Lazzard asked, raising his eyebrows.

"Vira*llon*," he snapped. "And I'd wager all of Span that it's more than what's in yours!"

Renna grinned at that and Trujo laughed.

"Let us be off. With any luck, the Mands in Tindin will know more about the state of the clocks by the time we reach that city." Virallon mounted his pony with a determined air.

"If we take the Alginock River route through the Tindin Ridge, we can get there faster," Lazzard said, brushing off the Scrall's insult. "It's not the easiest route, but I can guide you from above."

Renna stood up and reached for Stalwart's reins, desperately wishing they could lie and rest. The Tindin Ridge was still several days' ride away, and who knew what awaited them now, with the border open between Avid and Span?

The Envoy's horse had fallen sick at the start of his journey, which was why the poor man had been carrying out his mission on foot. It was decided that Lazzard could most easily get along without his steed, being able to fly for large periods of the day. The rest of the time, he could trade off riding behind anyone else.

So they bid goodbye to Endi as he mounted the Krimmer's surprised horse. Renna suspected the animal would enjoy having a more predictable rider. But as they turned to go, the Envoy called out to her, in the back of the company.

"My human friend! Did you say that you hail from Toom?"

"Yes!" She waited impatiently, as Stalwart tried to follow the others.

Endi frowned and shook his head. "I'm very sorry to tell you, but that village was destroyed just days ago by Jibbs and Spinners . . . I heard that there were few survivors."

Renna's blood froze. Her cloak shot out straight behind her.

Endi shook his head again in sympathy and bowed. Then he turned and rode away.

Home. Her . . . *home.*

The physical shock of the news about the clocks was nothing compared to the new horror that flashed through her.

Her mother! She hadn't been there to protect her!

She gasped. Then she half-slid, half-fell off Stalwart, startling him.

Someone called her name. Her cloak flapped helplessly at her sides.

Callin . . . His dear face floated before her eyes. He would've tried to save her mother—she knew he would have.

And Barrin! Her tough old teacher. Had he managed to survive?

"Renna?" Virallon asked, his tone exasperated.

Her companions had ridden back toward her and stood there, staring.

She tried to fight it, but the image of her mother lying bloodied on the ground slammed her in the gut. She vomited suddenly, Sallindar's herbs the only thing in her stomach.

"She is ill!" Dunn exclaimed.

Her throat burned and tears rushed from her stinging eyes. She could not bear this—she had to get away from the others. She could not show so much weakness.

Sobbing, she mounted her horse and slapped the reins, headed for the nearest grove of trees. Stalwart nickered in confusion and the others shouted after her.

She rode deep into the shade of the trees and then spilled off the saddle again. Stalwart whinnied and nosed at her. She stumbled to a large rock and sank down upon it, weeping in wretched, painful lurches.

The clocks be damned. Nothing mattered now . . . She took a deep breath, remembering that the Envoy had said there were survivors. Her mother might be living roughly with refugees. She struggled to think about where they would go, and who might help them. The closest neighbor to Toom was Rendir and it was likely to have been attacked as well.

She could head straight there and start the search. But it would take so long to reach—

A terrible realization struck her. When she accepted the mission from the Appon . . . she had agreed to continue no matter the cost.

Did that really mean she couldn't go find her own mother?

No. That was impossible.

Furious, she yanked the emblem from her cloak, tearing the fabric. She raised her arm to fling it away into the trees, the impulse as powerful as a storm.

But Sallindar materialized beside her.

She jumped, startled out of her spinning thoughts. It took a moment to realize that he hadn't manifested out of thin air. He had simply stepped up silently.

She threw him a miserable glare and turned away, wiping at her hot tears.

"Is it your family?" he asked, low.

She shuddered and nodded. Every breath

was a blade in her heart.

"Are they gone?"

"I don't know," she gasped. "But Toom was destroyed."

He sat down on the rock beside her, and she looked down at their two pairs of ravaged boots. They were nearly the same size, but his were fastened with something like silver wire, looped into a pattern.

"I saw the shock on your face when the Envoy spoke to you," he said gravely.

"I didn't want everyone to see me cry," she murmured and closed her hands over the badge in her lap. She hadn't wanted to be followed, but now that he was here, she was somehow glad. She couldn't bear the grief alone any better than she could with the group.

The sympathy in his voice was also a small coat of balm, like a single elderline leaf against a skin-crackling burn. They were silent for a long moment while she wept.

"I have only seen tears once before," he said quietly.

Renna blinked at him in disbelief. Then she remembered that most species did not cry. It was largely a human trait.

There was a sense of wonder in Sallindar's eyes, but also sadness.

"When I was returning from the Cartru Desert, the humans of Luftine in the Cold Mountains were struck by an avalanche."

She nodded. "I heard the story. You rescued them."

"Not all," he murmured. "I could have,

96

perhaps. But many of them got in the way, trying to help."

Renna sniffled, recalling his agreement with Trujo's description of her race as "feisty and foolish." She sighed heavily.

"Well, I'm sure it's an unpleasant sight. I'm sorry."

"Don't apologize for grief," he told her. He lifted the pendant on his necklace and held it out in his four-fingered hand. "This necklace holds a hair each from my mother, father, and sister. The connection we have is strained by distance, but this keeps it from breaking. I know they're safe because I would feel it otherwise."

Renna marveled at the smooth silver circle, with the smaller spheres inside.

"Where do they live?" she asked. Then she bit her lip, remembering how private his kind were.

"In and around the Askeye Woods, in the north," he replied, unperturbed. "My father made me this pendant because I travel so often."

So she had been right in thinking that Sallindar ventured out on his own. All that she knew of the Askeye was that it was cold and full of Vandids, fierce predators with thick fur and spines. It was a good place to live if one wanted to be left alone, but also a testament to the hardiness of Sallindar's people.

"If only I were a Tillen, I might know if my mother survived," she said wistfully.

"Instead, you must hope, with your strong heart." The words were simple, but he said them with such sincerity that, for a moment, it did give her hope. Perhaps it was too soon to give up.

She glanced at him sideways, curious despite her grief. It was the most she'd heard him speak and it felt flatteringly special. He seemed much more corporeal, sitting so close to her. She could see fine lines in his pale skin and his long hair was mussed and smelled of smoke.

But perhaps he would've comforted any of the others the same way, had they received terrible news. Not that it mattered one way or the other.

She had committed to this company and this mission. Both her mother and Callin would have insisted that she carry on—of that much she was certain. And Barrin, most of all, would goad her into keeping her promise.

She wiped her face again, knowing it would remain red and puffy for hours. *Let them all see it*, she thought grimly. *I am human indeed.*

Slowly, with numb fingers, she re-pinned her badge to her cloak.

"We better go back," she told Sallindar.

He tilted his head and didn't answer, listening to something Renna could not hear. Then his solemn face lit up.

"What is it?" she asked.

"I think you chose a special place to grieve, unknowingly." He stood up and gestured for her to follow.

Almost as soon as he did, she noticed an odd stillness in the air. Her misery had distracted her from it, but there was a kind of respectful quiet that made her feel like she was being observed. But why here? In this small grove of woods?

Her scalp tingled strangely as she followed him.

Then, deeper into the trees, she heard the flow of water. There was something unusual about the way it murmured and echoed; the sounds were like a chorus of subdued voices.

Sallindar parted a mass of ferns and suddenly, a secluded pool revealed itself, encircled by rocks and overhanging plants.

Renna gasped. The water was not blue or clear, but a blend of jewel tones—purples, reds, yellows, even white . . . ! Every color she could imagine and all the ones in between.

The different hues swam together in opposite directions, churning gently this way and that. The movement cast rainbows of mist into the air, as the light refracted upon the prism waters.

"A Swirl," Renna breathed. She stood motionless, overwhelmed by the uncanny beauty of the sight. "I can't believe it."

Soft voices drifted over the particolor liquid, rising from its surface and sinking slowly back into its depths. She listened, marvelling, and wondered if colors possessed voices in their unfinished form. Or were there spirits living in the Swirls as well? She couldn't remember the stories anymore.

She had never been so enchanted.

"It is lucky to find one," Sallindar said. "Some of my people believe that we originally emerged from the Swirls. But our known history doesn't go back that far."

She stared at him, remembering how the Indioc had given her the impression of young Tillen. Then she glanced up quickly, afraid that the relentless guardians might appear. But only tiny, flitting insects occupied the air.

"Do you think the Swirls will all be destroyed or corrupted? Now that the clocks are synced?" she asked sadly.

"They will if we delay any longer," Lazzard retorted.

Renna jumped in her skin. She turned to see him hovering behind them, his arms crossed.

"Despite all my knowledge of your flawed race, human, I never imagined that *you* would run off without a word to see a Swirl."

She rolled her eyes at the splintered ice in his voice. Of course, he was convinced she had sneaked off to try to become immortal.

"No, Lazzard. I didn't even know it was here," she told him wearily. "I ran off because . . . I received some bad news from Endi, something personal. But I'll be all right. Let's go."

The Krimmer frowned, confused, but he said nothing more.

From inside his tunic, Sallindar produced a small pouch with a stopper. Renna watched him crouch and fill it with the brilliant liquid from the Swirl. Alarmed, she looked up at Lazzard, but he had already floated back through the trees.

"Is that safe?" she asked. "What if the Indioc come after us?"

Sallindar shook his head and tucked the pouch away.

"How do you know?"

He gazed at the water for a long moment, his eyes gleaming. Renna suddenly wondered if he understood the murmuring voices.

"I don't think you stumbled upon this place by accident," he said. "I have a feeling that this

Swirl wanted to be found."

Chapter Nine

Skink surveyed the filth that surrounded him with immense pride. He had no way of knowing if this was the sort of lair that Lugis would've made, but it suited him nonetheless. He sat upon a throne-like pile of bones, brought to him by his newly acquired pack of Enja: the massive, blue dog-demons that lay curled about in puddles of saliva and bits of regurgitated meat.

The floors of the clock chamber no longer shone with the polish that magic had upheld for thousands of years. But there were new pieces of art in the chamber: two rather unusual statues. The moment that Skink had matched up the clocks, the Clock Keeper he'd bargained with simply froze in place. He seemed to shut down like a machine.

The other one had done the same, somewhere down the spiraling steps. Delighted, Skink had brought him up into the chamber, and placed them side by side.

He had not even known that once they failed at their single responsibility, they would all but cease to exist. It was both amusing to him and—distantly, somewhere inside—a bit sad. He had planned to keep his side of the bargain, happily removing them both from the tower as long as they left him alone with his prize. But now they were extra prizes.

Made of gold, silver, and iron—and Elevad of the Appon's unfathomable magic—the clocks themselves ticked quietly at the chamber's center. They were as tall as Skink, and so solidly built, they were heavy as horses. Like hourglasses, their sides narrowed beneath their lustrous faces, and then widened again below. Upon the clock on the left, the word SPAN was carved in intricate gold letters, and the clock on the right bore the word AVID, painted black.

When Skink was not admiring them, he smiled at the small portal shimmering outside one of the windows whenever it caught his eye. It was the hole he had made in the tower's shield to prove himself to the Clock Keeper and seal the deal.

No matter how proud he was of his wily intelligence, he knew it was the old magic that swelled and ebbed inside him that had gotten him this far. It was a wholly unexpected side effect of the shapeshifting gift granted him by a disreputable magician in exchange for his precious wings. Those he suspected had been crushed into a powder by now, to be used in complicated spells.

Before that ancient power bubbled up to the surface, Skink had never imagined anything more than shaping himself to look like Lugis, his idol and magnificent ancestor. But with the discovery of old magic inside him came the possibility to . . . actually . . . *follow* in Lugis's footsteps! To recreate the glorious chaos and destruction in the legends!

His plan was swiftly forged, along with the decision to delay his transformation into Lugis until the dream had come to fruition. Since that day, he had appeared most often as Skink, a lizard-man that could wend its way in and out of the underworld of Iddlar. He was Skink and Skink was he.

Luckily, the old magic had also given him enough regeneration to survive one Clock Keeper's assault. He could not have survived another.

Outside, at the base of the tower, a horde of monsters built their rough camps, cavorting amongst themselves. They were challenging each other, destroying the weak, consuming the dead, and forging brief, violent alliances. He could hear their strange wild cries and feel the tower tremble as they thundered back and forth across the ground.

They would not leave; they were attracted to his power.

The Avidian creatures had come pouring in through invisible cracks as soon as he'd moved the clocks' hands into place, potency crackling from his fingers. The moment had been as delicious as he'd anticipated: The ancient timepieces vibrated in protest for a moment. Then they each struck a chilling tone somewhere deep inside their magical workings.

The chamber shook as if the tower were caught in a powerful windstorm. Strange sparks flooded the air and blinded Skink. He staggered backward and choked . . . as the air itself *changed*. The light from the windows dimmed as if a translucent lid had covered the sky.

It was magnificent. It was the most thrilling moment of his long, miserable life.

Now he sat clicking his claws together, biding his time. First the beasts from Avid must be organized, and their obedience proven. Then he would send them out on excursions to bend all of Span to his will.

Oh, the mighty Lugis had failed in the end, but this time there was no Santir. No savior to surprise him at the last moment.

So now, there was no more reason for delay. Skink grinned slowly from ear to ear. Then his body swelled and stretched in size.

In moments, he was the perfect image of his diabolical ancestor.

*   *   *

Renna drew Stalwart up short at the sight of the Alginock River ahead. It was three times as wide as she'd imagined, and much more powerful. The water smashed its way through the lightly wooded land, dragging dead trees and boulders along with it. White froth and spray sparkled in the air, but the powerful roar of the rapids made that beauty ominous.

"Thank Span we don't have to cross that." Virallon was barely audible.

"It doesn't look difficult to me!" Lazzard called out smugly, sitting behind Trujo. Of course, the Krimmer could fly straight over it, if needed.

Virallon fixed his sharp gaze upon Lazzard. Woolly brows knitted, he seemed to be deciding whether to say something.

"If only we had wings," he said finally, pointedly.

Lazzard's smirk disappeared into a stony expression. Renna didn't understand the comment, but she didn't care. She had been struggling to keep thoughts of her mother at bay. They were squeezed into a mass inside her: an aching knot of fear and guilt.

"If only we were all Krimmers! They don't even need wings," Trujo said, oblivious to Lazzard's tension.

"We do not have to cross it," Dunn said, glancing curiously from Lazzard to Virallon. "But as it cuts through the Tindin Ridge, I understand we must follow it."

Lazzard nodded. He and Trujo led the way, steering their large steed alongside the rushing water.

Beyond the massive rock formation known as the Tindin Ridge was the great city of Tindin itself, home of the warrior sect, the Mands. Renna knew they must be highly agitated now that the tower had been breached.

The Mands were Hawind, distant relatives of the Heuwit. Whereas Dunn was somewhat like a human crossed with a deer, a Hawind was like a man-cougar, a trait that made them powerful fighters. They were tall and well-muscled, covered in thick shaggy fur that was often golden-colored.

The Mands were an odd group, however. They considered themselves the second line of defense for the Time Tower after the Clock Keepers, since Tindin was its closest city. But they abused this self-appointed position in ways that made them unpopular, including sparking an altercation with the avian serpents known as the

Winged Alka, by ordering that the airspace above the tower always be kept clear.

The demand was unnecessary, considering that inhabitation of the moorland around the tower had been long forbidden by the Appon, and the second closest dwelling place was the city of Luder on the other side of the moors to the east.

It was that skirmish that had led the Winged Alka to move into Tillen territory and attempt to claim it for themselves. Remembering Trujo's story about Sallindar and the Winged Alka, Renna wondered if that territory had been in the Askeye Woods or if he had travelled to help others of his kind.

"As far as wings go, it is odd that certain kinds are practical and others are ornamental," Virallon mused aloud, watching Lazzard. Renna frowned, wondering what he was getting at. "And then there are those that mark a specific *lineage*."

The Krimmer's back stiffened, but he did not turn around.

"Virallon," Sallindar warned.

"What is he talking about?" Trujo asked, looking back at the Scrall.

"Are you speaking of the descendants of Lugis?" Dunn asked curiously. "I have heard that even now, they sometimes bear his vestigial wings."

Renna sucked in her breath, light dawning. The nubs on Lazzard's back . . . that he'd been so ashamed of . . .

She looked at Sallindar, who was frowning at Virallon.

Now she recalled having heard the same thing as Dunn, years ago, about the long-diluted bloodline of Lugis. Charming and manipulative, he had sired many children before turning his attention to Avid and the clocks. Any sign of his lineage was a shameful mark to bear, so she could well imagine why someone would have those wings removed.

"The wings of his descendents are said to be so difficult to remove that the stubs are often left behind," Virallon said calmly.

"But it must be worth the trouble, since many would judge those individuals harshly," Dunn replied.

"Rightly so, in certain cases," Virallon declared.

At this, Lazzard finally turned, piercing him with a glare.

"Well, there can't be many left," Trujo said.

"Or any at all," Lazzard growled suddenly. The Ralgir flinched in surprise. "Surely they were all strangled at birth!" the Krimmer shouted.

He sprang into the air and hovered, dark fury uncoiling like smoke around him.

"If not, they should be tortured their entire lives for their ancestor's actions!" he spat down at them. "Distrusted forever!"

Virallon met his glare with equal intensity, their eyes locked for several moments.

"Perhaps they should," the Scrall said coldly.

Something seemed to snap inside of Lazzard. His features compressed and expanded.

"Oh, yes, they should!" he cried out. "Until they turn *mad* like my cousin!"

Then he shot away like a cannon ball. It was so fast that his figure dwindled instantly to nothing.

Renna stared after him, the bitterness in his words seeping into her bones.

"We saw the evidence on his back in the woods," Virallon told Dunn and Trujo triumphantly.

"His bloodline is not our concern," Sallindar said with sudden force.

"Not our concern?" Virallon threw up his arms in disgust. "We are traveling to undo the same evil committed by his very ancestor!"

"But that doesn't mean that he sympathizes with Lugis," Renna insisted.

"How can we trust him?" Virallon countered. "He should not be a part of this mission!"

Renna said nothing, doubts growing inside her. It did seem inappropriate to have a descendant of Lugis among them. She admired Sallindar for being so ready to disregard it.

"The Appon summoned him just as they did the rest of us," Dunn said uncertainly. His brow was furrowed, his antlers low.

"Perhaps they aren't aware of his lineage," Virallon said, but he sounded unconvinced himself. The Appon would have thoroughly investigated each of their champions.

"Hold on . . . *Lazzard* is a descendant of Lugis?" Trujo scratched one of his pointed ears, confused.

"Where did he go when he disappeared back there in the Aggard Forest?" Virallon prompted him. "How do we know he wasn't sending a signal? Reporting our progress to someone?"

"To whom?" Renna asked.

"To whomever is waiting for us at the Time

Tower!"

"But he's a Krimmer," Trujo protested.

Virallon rolled his yellow eyes. "Oh, come, Trujo! There are many mixed species that *appear* to be pure-blooded—"

"Enough." Dunn's face had darkened, and Renna remembered his dislike of arguments.

The Scrall scowled at him but said no more. His expression was a strange mix of triumph and worry.

They followed the river in a troubled silence for a long while. Renna glanced up at every passing bird, expecting to see Lazzard, but he did not return.

Perhaps he would not this time.

The sky colors faded into evening, briefly turning everything red, including the tumultuous water. In her head, Renna heard the voices of the old fishermen back in Toom: *"A red river is a sign of bad luck."* She shook her head, frowning. Barrin would have told her that was nonsense.

"I hope someone else besides Lazzard knows the way," Trujo commented.

"We just follow the river, Ralgir," Virallon said impatiently.

"What about the way through the Ridge?" Dunn asked. The Krimmer would have found the easiest path, directing them from above; that was why he had suggested the route.

The Scrall frowned and said nothing.

"Lazzard will come back," Renna told them. "He made the same promise to the Appon as the rest of us."

If she had not left to find her poor mother, then surely, he wouldn't abandon them out of anger.

110

Then again, she couldn't imagine the kind of discrimination and distrust the Krimmer had faced in his lifetime. She had never seen anyone as furious as Virallon had made him either.

Night fell and their missing companion had still not returned. In the dark, Sallindar alone could see the Tindin Ridge approaching. The Alginock widened, rushing through the spindly trees between the riders and the rough water.

"Should we stop for the night and pass through the Ridge tomorrow?" Renna called out.

The others slowed their horses and looked at each other, considering. The urgency of their mission had increased significantly, but it was true that the darkness would impair them.

Virallon shook his head with a sudden sigh. "We have no time to spare. We must push on."

It wasn't long before the Ridge itself loomed over them, and the river seeped into the path where they rode, pushing them outward. Stalwart snorted in disgust at having wet hooves, and Renna could not blame him. The spray from the dark water was cold.

Dunn produced a lantern from his pack and soon threw a flickering gleam over their faces.

"Sallindar! Can you lead us?" he asked.

The Tillen nodded and rode ahead. It was only then that Renna realized he had been riding close to her ever since they left the Swirl. Her pulse quickened suddenly, frustratingly. She reminded herself that he was simply concerned about her and her grief.

The rock formation faced them now like a massive city gate. The width was almost more impressive than the height, which was why alternate routes that skirted it would have cost them too much time. The irregular line of rock turrets was silhouetted forbiddingly against the sky.

Sallindar took the lantern from Dunn and dropped soundlessly from his horse. In the circle of light, he began climbing rocks, casting wild shadows over the water.

Renna could just make out that the river slogged its way through the jagged ridge in various forked streams. They just had to find one wide enough to pass through with the horses.

Sallindar returned after a moment, his pants wet up to the knee.

"I found a route, but it's treacherous. Slippery."

The rest of them dismounted to lead the horses. The rising ridge was not so steep that a strong horse couldn't be led upward, but the passage would be slow and the animals unhappy.

"Can my beast get through?" Trujo asked.

The Tillen nodded.

"What kind of creature is that anyway?" Renna asked Trujo as they began an awkward ascent.

The animal's wide face looked at the uneven ground in dismay, but it followed.

"Don't ask me," he said, patting its tough hide. "It belongs to the Appon."

Sallindar gave them such a withering, disappointed look that Renna almost laughed.

"That's an Aloppin," he admonished. "There are large herds of them in the Acrin."

"Oh," Renna said, mystified.

"What on Span is the Acrin?" Trujo asked.

"The Acrin Basin!" Virallon huffed behind them. His pony was balking at climbing the wet rocks, but the Scrall dragged it along. "Thought to be inhospitable for hundreds of years . . . but later known for unusual plant life . . . some of it useful."

"Much like the Cartru Desert," Dunn commented. "You must travel a great deal, Tillen."

Stalwart whinnied as a rush of icy water soaked their feet. Renna gasped at the shock and hurried up onto the next cluster of rocks. Virallon swore and hissed; the water had reached above his knees.

"How much further?" Renna asked, shivering. No one answered.

It was increasingly difficult to drag the horses up the rocks, but after half an hour of struggling, she saw open air above the dark water ahead. Instead of overhanging rock, the night sky patterns shone faintly out of a black haze. A brief memory struck her of night skygazing on her back in a field with Callin. She shook it off, focusing on her footing.

The river was gushing through a break in the ridge about the width of a carriage. On either side, the water surged into small caves and tunnels as well, taking every opportunity to squeeze through the rock.

Relieved at the sight, Renna pulled Stalwart up, hoof by reluctant hoof, squashing into muddy streams between the stones. For several long moments, the only sounds were the river whisking and the grunts of her companions.

Then Virallon screamed.

Renna jumped and Stalwart snorted, tugging backward. A loud splash followed—the Scrall's head and waving arms flew by in the river.

"Virallon!" she gasped.

It was so fast, even Sallindar reacted too slowly.

"Catch him!" Dunn boomed.

Trujo plunged heavily into the water and sloshed around wildly. Sallindar swung the lantern. The light caught Virallon's gray head rushing down another inlet.

"There!" Renna shouted.

He disappeared into a dark cave inside the ridge. It was across the water, on the other side of the open passage.

Trujo plowed his way toward the cave as the others jumped into the freezing water. Renna sank up to her chest in the dark, miserable flood. The cold shock stole her breath; her arms and legs were struck numb. The current swept her into Dunn's side, and she clung to him, surprised at its strength. The water came up only to his hips, and he strode powerfully against the flow.

Sallindar was somehow swimming against it with one arm and holding the lantern up with the other. He reached the cave first. Then Dunn and Trujo ducked to splash into it behind him. Still hanging on to Dunn, Renna's legs dragged roughly against stone and mud under the water. She got to her feet, half-running, half-swimming.

Her thoughts were spiralling darkly. *He could've drowned by now! We've lost him! It's too late!*

Sallindar's lantern flashed, revealing how

the cave widened into a large room with a high ceiling. The river pooled inside it, tendrils slipping out through openings in different directions. The rushing water echoed loudly against the rock walls.

Directly ahead, the rock was covered in a thick web of algae or fungus.

"Take this!" the Tillen rasped, swinging the lantern at Trujo. Then he plunged under the water.

"Do you see him?" Renna gasped.

"No." Dunn's voice reverberated, shaking the walls.

There was no sign of either of them for several awful moments.

Then Sallindar resurfaced, and his arm was around Virallon.

"He's got him!" Trujo crowed.

He plucked the tiny Scrall from Sallindar and set him down on the ledge above the water. Renna scrambled up beside him, shivering violently. Virallon lay still with his eyes closed, his hat long vanished into the river. His gray hair streamed water out beside him.

"Is he alive?"

"Is he breathing?"

The webbing on the wall swayed in the force of their echoes.

"His heart is beating," Sallindar said.

Trujo rolled Virallon onto his side and thumped his small back. Renna held her breath, as the Scrall lay there limply.

Then suddenly he choked and spat up water.

She heaved a sigh and sat back on her heels. They still had their Scrall.

Trujo cheered, the sound ringing through the

cave. Virallon coughed up more water and gasped, opening his yellow eyes.

Relief eased Renna's muscles for just a moment – then everything clenched up again in the cold. She thought of the poor horses outside across the water, shivering and confused.

Sallindar's pouch of Swirl water bobbed up in the pool and he jumped in to retrieve it. He climbed back out as Trujo helped Virallon sit up.

With a start, Sallindar stared at the wall above them. He drew his sword as the growth across it suddenly stirred.

"Help," a small voice sprang from within. "Help me!"

Startled, Dunn and Trujo grabbed their weapons. Virallon flinched and shrank back down to the cave floor.

"Who are you?" Renna asked, clutching her staff.

Up close, she could see that there were several large shapes within the webbing. One was struggling to move, fastened to the wall.

"Trapped . . . Cut me out," the voice murmured. "Cut me out!"

Sallindar slashed the coarse strands on both sides of the moving shape, but the trapped individual did not fall free. There were more layers. Trujo raised his axe, but the Tillen shook his head; it was too risky for the victim. Renna grasped hold of the sticky threads as he sawed at them with his blade.

"What animal makes a web like this?" Dunn asked, turning his antlered head to look around the cave.

116

Virallon coughed hoarsely and cleared his throat. "Nothing good," he muttered. "We should leave."

An Idgian's spines emerged first from the trap, and then came her bulbous head, gasping for air. She was very weak and blinked her violet eyes in the lantern light.

Renna grimaced at the rough, sticky webbing in her hands, but she pulled and tore as much as she could. Sallindar moved to the other bulges in the trap and began slicing around them. Trujo eyed the rest of the cave with Dunn, brandishing his axe.

"I think the Scrall is right! I don't want to meet this web-spitter," he declared, his voice booming around the walls.

The Idgian wiggled herself free and slipped down to the ground, panting. She curled into a defensive spine-ball for a moment. Then she stretched out flat, limply. Renna peeled the last of the sticky trap from her shredded clothing and saw that she had one long-ago withered leg.

The Idgian gestured at Sallindar and shook her head.

"All dead . . . poisoned!" she told him. "I am lame . . . It did not need to bite me."

"Let us leave this miserable place!" Virallon crawled to his feet, shivering.

Sallindar stopped and waved his lantern at the other walls. Renna saw from his face that he could hear something.

"Let's go," she said, helping the Idgian up.

Dunn lifted the creature and placed her across his shoulders. Trujo scooped up Virallon and did the same. Renna slid back into the water with them, her teeth chattering. Sallindar swam ahead toward the cave mouth, the lantern aloft.

Then something large slid past Renna underwater.

She shrieked and tried to climb up Trujo's back. He hollered and spun around.

"Something's in the water!" she screamed.

Dunn gasped and stumbled aside— something had rubbed against him too.

"It's back!" the Idgian wailed.

Renna yanked up her soaking hood and slipped into her Umbra state, focusing hard.

Sallindar turned slowly in the water, taut as a wire, his sword in one hand and lantern in the other.

"What underwater brute spins a web?" Virallon demanded. "What madness is this?"

He did not wonder long. In a heartbeat, a giant mass burst through the surface. Renna gaped as the grotesque creature wavered in the air. It resembled an enormous tongue—with feelers at its very top. It bent weirdly in the middle and the feelers faced them, waving.

Then its skin split and pinchers the size of swords emerged.

The Idgian screamed.

The monster dived straight for her.

Renna cracked her staff across its face, knocking the pinchers aside. Trujo struck his axe into its slimy side—it writhed, tilting itself backward. Then it crashed back into the water.

Sallindar stabbed at the surface as ripples flew past him. Then the beast shot up between him and the cave mouth. It bobbed at him, pinchers snapping. He parried and backed away, nearly dropping the lantern.

"Don't even let it scratch you!" the Idgian warned. "Poison!"

Dunn fired an arrow into the beast's belly. It doubled over and sank into the water again. Sallindar held up the light, his eyes wary.

The fiend could bite them unseen under the surface.

"Get out of the water!" Renna shouted, plunging back toward the ledge behind them.

Trujo growled and stumbled suddenly. He smashed his axe down into the water. Blood seeped upward to the surface.

The leviathan writhed, churning water and splashing blood into Renna's face. She had just managed to climb up the rock ledge before the beast flung itself upon it. With a scream, she jumped back into the pool.

The beast pulsed and oozed dark blood, flopping like a snake.

"Watch the lantern!" Dunn warned, as the water splashed wildly.

Virallon flung up his hands and shouted, "Ellarune idd—"

A cannon blast of webbing from the creature cut him off. Renna ducked underwater—into that silent blackness that offered no relief. Then she bobbed up again as fast as she could.

Trujo and Virallon were struggling in a net of the sprayed webbing.

Dunn fired an arrow, but it missed the swaying beast. The thing splashed into the water, and everyone back-swam frantically.

Salendar reached out and slashed open the web around Trujo. Enraged, the Ralgir started plunging his axe repeatedly into the water, with Virallon hanging on to his shoulders.

He made contact and the monster emerged again. Gushing blood, it gnashed its pinchers in all directions.

Renna jammed her staff into one of its wounds. It shuddered in agony. Then it lunged at her—

Then Dunn shot it straight between its pinchers.

It gurgled a miserable cry. A powerful tremor shot through it, churning the water madly.

"Watch out!"

"Get back!"

Renna slipped and slid under, swallowing a mouthful of water. Then she scrambled back to her feet.

The creature whipped itself back and forth for several long moments. It tossed the water violently, slamming everyone backward into hard rock.

Then finally, it crashed back below the surface. From the depths came a strangely beautiful, echoing sigh.

Renna stood frozen, holding her staff above the water. No one else moved, still in shock.

Then the lantern sputtered out, swallowing them all in darkness.

"It might have a mate!" Virallon yelled.

Renna spun and floundered toward the cave entrance. She heard Trujo cursing as the slimy webbing hindered him. Amid deafening splashes and echoes, they finally emerged into the night air.

Across the span of open water that greeted them, Stalwart whinnied and reared in relief. The other horses snorted and stamped, barely visible in the dark.

Sallindar swam ahead and reached them first. Exhausted, Renna held onto Trujo's webbing as he lumbered after him.

It was then she noticed, her breath catching in her throat, that the Ralgir's pants were torn—blood was floating up to the surface.

Chapter Ten

"Either an Alithuwin or some class of Bynerdi. Or a Vellor, I suppose . . . None of these sighted since the days of Lugis, mind you!"

As he spoke, Virallon tore at the web strands dangling from him. Sallindar was relighting the lantern as Trujo set the Scroll down on the rocks.

Then Trujo wavered, frowning. A deep calf wound was visible through the rip in his pants.

"It scratched him!" Renna cried out, pointing. "Look at his leg!"

The others froze in the midst of wringing themselves out. Sallindar shone the lantern on Trujo. The Ralgir winced down at his bloody trousers and sat heavily on one of the rocks.

"It hurts a lot more than it should," he told them.

Renna's gut twisted as he tore the pant leg away. His skin around the gash was already turning blue and swelling.

"I'm so sorry," the Idgian said, shaking her head.

"What is the poison?" Sallindar asked Virallon quickly.

"I don't know!" he exclaimed, getting to his feet.

The two of them examined Trujo's calf, Renna and Dunn crowding behind them.

"It spreads fast," the Idgian wept.

"We must act swiftly, whatever we do!" Dunn's voice was thick with fear.

Trujo eyed them in a silent panic.

Renna thought suddenly of the weaver's son at home that had been stung by a flying Biddel—his arm had swollen and turned different colors.

"I have no herbs for this," Sallindar told them, his face grim.

"I . . . I will try a few different spells," Virallon sputtered. "But without knowing what type of—"

"Cut off his leg!" Renna blurted. That was how the boy in Toom had survived; the healer had chopped off his arm. "We don't have time to guess! He's dying!"

Virallon stared at her, aghast, but Sallindar nodded. He sprang up and grabbed Trujo's axe. The Scrall backed away as Dunn clamped his arms around Trujo to hold him steady.

"What?" the Ralgir demanded, confused.

Renna whirled, covering her face. The Idgian cried out.

There was a grisly *thunk.*

Then Trujo's howl made the horses scream. Renna dropped to her knees in horror.

What had they done? At *her* suggestion? Would it even save him?

She expected another blow, but none came—the Ralgir hollered again instead.

"May all of Alabass crush your bones into powder!"

"Quick!" Sallindar shouted.

She turned back to see Dunn digging for bandages from his pack. There would not be enough.

"My rain cloak," she murmured and ran to Stalwart, who tried to pull away, frightened. With her knife, she tore off a long strip of the cloak and passed it to Sallindar.

Trujo was jerking violently in shock and pain. His tree-trunk leg had been severed in one blow under the knee.

It was incredible that Sallindar had possessed the strength.

Renna watched numbly as he tied the strip of her cloak around the leg, knotting it fiercely. Dunn poured river water over the laceration, refilled his pouch and did it again. Then Sallindar packed the wound with the elderline leaves he had saved, and bound it.

The Ralgir's calf and foot, lying where it had fallen between two rocks, bubbled white inside the poisoned wound. But the discoloration had not spread to his knee or thigh.

Trujo moaned, staring first at his foot and then back at his bandaged stump.

"Did we stop it from spreading?" Renna asked shakily, looking from Sallindar to Dunn.

"I believe so," Sallindar said. He looked at her in quiet admiration and she blushed. He had done all the work; she had merely thought quickly. If Trujo was saved, they had done it together.

Holding his gaze, her mind flashed back to

124

him circling in the water with sword and lantern high. He was truly magnificent.

She, on the other hand, had tried to climb up the Ralgir's back when the monster brushed her leg.

"First poisoned and then butchered," Trujo growled. He glared at them all with bleary eyes, arms hanging limply at his sides. "The clocks be damned! I didn't agree to this!"

How in Span is he supposed to fight? Renna thought, her shoulders slumped.

He was alive though. The strength of his disgust and the healthy color of his red-brown skin made that clear.

"We were crossing the ridge there because it was the fastest way into Tindin," the Idgian told them suddenly, hoarse with grief. "Our village was destroyed by those giant grasshoppers . . . My son wanted to seek protection from the Mands." She sobbed. "My son!"

Renna's heart ached as the poor thing buried her head in her arms.

"Jibbs," Virallon muttered.

"You're lucky we found you," Trujo told the Idgian in a tired voice. "You can thank Virallon for nearly drowning himself."

"I *fell*," the Scrall snapped.

"Are the Mands offering protection?" Dunn asked the Idgian.

"That's what we heard," she murmured. "They are the only ones."

"I am so sorry," Renna said, her voice shaking. "We'll take you to a safe place in Tindin, I promise."

"You'll have to do that for me too," Trujo

125

rumbled. "I'm not much use now."

"Do not be so hasty," Dunn told him. "The Mands may know of a physician that can fit you with a false limb."

"Yes," Virallon said, nodding. "The wound should be cauterized as well."

Trujo snorted. "Poisoned and butchered and burned!"

There was nothing else to do but help the Ralgir back onto his Aloppin and set the Idgian in Lazzard's place behind him.

At the thought of the Krimmer, Renna looked up automatically, cursing him for his absence.

They had lost one champion and permanently maimed another.

*   *   *

The morning sky hues were just appearing when they reached the city gates. The colors seemed even duller than before, and the light from them weak. Renna blinked repeatedly, feeling as if gauze were covering her eyes.

Tindin was the largest site they had come across yet, its stone city wall rising nearly as high as the Tindin Ridge. They rode up to the double gates and halted, gazing up toward the top of the imposing wall. It bore elaborate symbols representing both the ridge and the Time Tower.

After a moment, two guards atop the wall looked down at the travelers. One was a Rydit and the other a Galopine, his long feelers tumbling out of his helmet like braids.

"We have come to see the Mands!" Dunn told them, his impressive voice floating upward.

"You don't look like refugees," the Rydit called down.

"No, they look like trouble," the Galopine said with a snort.

It occurred to Renna then just how rough she and her companions appeared: damp, bandaged, and filthy, but well-armed. They were also exhausted and scowling.

"We've had enough trouble since the clocks were changed," the Rydit told them.

Virallon, whose woolly hair had dried comically outward, drew himself up with as much dignity as possible.

"We are emissaries of the Appon!" he said hoarsely. "Champions sent to restore the clocks!"

Renna's eyebrows shot up at the word *champions*. How Lazzard would've laughed! She glanced at Sallindar and to her surprise, he grinned.

"The Mands should be expecting us!" Dunn added.

The two guards frowned at each other. Renna knew that the sect was not popular among the rest of the Tindinians, even if they were helpful allies against Avidian invaders.

"We've got Appon badges!" Trujo bellowed. "Damn you! Let us in!"

"All right, all right! There's one of the Shags here now." The Rydit turned and shouted down the other side of the wall to someone below.

There was a long pause before the heavy gates were cranked open. Then a tall Mand—clearly the "Shag" —was visible, awaiting them on the other side.

As they rode through, Renna looked up at the under-stones of the great wall overhead. The only other city she had traveled to was Laribb, when her father was still alive. She had only been ten years old, but the many smells and sounds flashed back to her: petrichor, hooves and wheels on cobblestone, clangs of metal, the hum of voices, and occasional shouts.

The Mand stood regarding the travelers with his bright cat eyes, yellow fur ruffling in the breeze. His pelt squeezed out from every joint in his polished armor, the breastplate of which was carved with a fist inside a circle. He was an imposing and solemn sight.

"For love of Span," he said formally.

"And defense against Avid," Virallon responded in the same tone.

"I see you bear an emblem from the Appon," the Mand continued. "You must be the Scrall who can reset the clocks. Our lords will be most relieved to see you! Follow me."

He turned and loped away at a remarkably rapid pace. Renna had just made a move to dismount, but she changed her mind as Virallon urged his pony after him.

The group clopped along behind the Mand, their heads turning to take in the sights of the city. The Galopines that made up the most of Tindin's population did not look up as the travelers rode through, their feelers bobbing and floating as they went on with the day's work.

The distinctive appendages were like tentacles or long hair that moved of its own accord.

Renna found it interesting to watch.

Rydits and others were rebuilding a large structure that had recently burned, half of it blackened and open to the elements. The guards had mentioned trouble; Renna looked around for other signs of attacks, and spotted telltale piles of rubble, strands of rising black smoke . . . weapons held close and faces alert.

It reminded her of the Idgian, who was quietly clinging to Trujo with her front legs. Renna knew she was too overwhelmed by shock and grief to speak up. She spurred Stalwart after the Mand and hailed him.

"Sir, we have a survivor with us from an attack at the ridge," she told him. "Is there somewhere we can take her?"

He nodded without slowing his pace. "The theatre has been made into a shelter for those who have lost their homes." He pointed toward a domed building, visible above the rooftops.

"Let's go there first then," Renna said, turning to Virallon who rode beside her.

"We don't have time to escort her," he said briskly. "We already have to request a physician for Trujo." Turning to the Ralgir, he added, "Set her down and let her make her way there."

Trujo slowed his Aloppin, but he frowned reluctantly. The Idgian said nothing, her face pale.

"She is lame, remember?" Renna told Virallon.

"This is not our concern. The Mand Lords are waiting for us!" the Scrall declared.

Renna's temper flared, but she struggled to quell it, realizing they were all out of humor. The

Scrall was also attempting to appear as their leader in front of the Mands, so she knew that he resented her questioning him.

Their guide had slowed to simply a fast walk, and now he was watching her and the Scrall.

"The theatre is not far, Virallon," she said calmly. "It will only take a few moments."

His eyes narrowed into angry, yellow slits. "We saved her life! We don't owe her anything further. We must stop this corruption at its source!"

"We will!" Renna exclaimed. "But I promised her that we would take her someplace safe!"

Virallon yanked on the reins and spun his small horse.

"Trujo, set the Idgian down!" he commanded. "Unsurprisingly, the human is projecting her own, personal grief onto this creature. She has forgotten her duty to the Appon."

Renna was briefly stunned by his words. Then flames engulfed her vision. Fury flashed through her, and her cloak whipped out into the air.

Sallindar put a hand up toward her, but she barely acknowledged it.

"Forgotten my *duty?*" she shouted. "How dare you? Did I abandon our mission when I learned about my *mother?* Am I not still here, you river-soaked fool?"

"Stop this bickering," Dunn said sternly, but the Scrall's face darkened like a bruised plum.

"I lost my family decades ago, human!" he roared. "Everyone I've ever loved was killed in some ridiculous conflict or another!" His voice was suddenly strange and thick. "Do you want accolades for enduring what *thousands* experience?"

Renna stared at him, taken aback. Somewhere inside those words was an agony that she had never imagined Virallon could feel.

Sadly, the outburst reminded her of Lazzard, whose own pain the Scrall had provoked and disparaged.

Stunned silence abounded after that.

Renna hunched in her saddle, avoiding the Mand's disapproving cat eyes. It was no surprise that the Tindinians were staring at them now.

"I will take the Idgian to the theatre." Sallindar rode up alongside Trujo and held out his hand. "The rest of you go on and I'll rejoin you."

He locked eyes with Renna as the Idgian took his arm and crawled down to his horse. Renna gave him a small, grateful smile.

"Perhaps you need rest and repast before meeting with our lords," the Mand suggested quietly.

Virallon said nothing, the color in his face fading.

"Perhaps," Dunn replied.

*   *   *

Sallindar returned just as the champions, all but Trujo, were finishing their bowls of soup in a long, high-ceilinged room in the Mands' Great Hall. Renna handed him a bowl and a mug of strong ale, both of which had warmed her insides and relaxed her sore muscles. He accepted it with a nod and sat close beside her.

The Ralgir was with a doctor that the Mands

had summoned.

The sounds of a lecture drifted into the room from a nearby chamber. There was a droning voice followed by repeated affirmations.

"We were discussing whether to search for Lazzard," Dunn informed Sallindar.

"Trujo thinks he may have gotten himself injured or trapped somewhere," Renna told him.

Sallindar nodded and drank his soup in one long, but silent, gulp.

Renna looked at Virallon, whose mood had been mollified by the food and rest.

"Even if he wasn't a spy, which is highly unlikely, he left us of his own accord," he said mildly. "He abandoned his . . . promised duty to the Appon."

He avoided Renna's eyes as he spoke, and she understood that he regretted his earlier words. He would never apologize for them, but he wouldn't broach the subject again.

Some of the Scrall's sharp edges had softened in the past hour, after his explosion. His shouted admission made his irascible manner a little more understandable to Renna, even if he did struggle with empathy.

Before the Mand guard had left them to eat and rest, she asked him for news about survivors from Toom. He had heard none, but he promised to request that an Envoy be sent. Eternally grateful, she gave him the names of her loved ones, hardly daring to hope.

"It is difficult to track someone who travels by air," Dunn said now, wiping his bowl clean.

"I suppose we could search for a fallen

Krimmer," Renna said. "But where would we start? We don't know how far off he flew."

The doors at the end of the room opened and she turned to look. Trujo thumped in slowly, a Mand with tan fur accompanying him. The Ralgir's lower leg was replaced by a battered metal column, strapped to his knee with a leather harness. It looked like a section of armor or shield that had been hammered into the right shape by a blacksmith. Despite the fast work, the piece was well-made, as wide across as his leg and sturdy enough not to be hacked through in battle.

Trujo was scowling, however, as he lurched toward them.

"Is it heavy?" Dunn asked.

"No, Heuwit, it's just not my leg," he retorted. He lifted it carefully and waved it side to side, balancing on one foot. He could still bend his knee, but he was quite unsteady as he walked around the table. "This will slow me down in a fight."

"Ralgirs aren't known for their speed in battle," Virallon said.

From what Renna had seen of Trujo's combat style, she knew the Scrall was right. Inexhaustible strength was his specialty, not speed or agility. The only real issue would be if they had to flee or give chase.

"Are you saying I was always slow?" he asked indignantly.

"No, no," Virallon amended.

The others nodded quickly. Then Renna grinned, remembering her first conversation with the Ralgir.

"Just a clumsy lout," she reminded him.

He snorted and reached for a mug of ale.

Shortly afterward, they entered a circular meeting room at the center of the building. Inside it sat the eight, aged Mand lords, gathered at a crescent-shaped table. They all wore necklaces bearing the symbol of the fist in a circle, but their fur varied in shades of gray and white. They wore plated armor as well, but it was obviously older than the guard's and not in recent use.

The room was unadorned and simple, with one large window covered in a sheer black curtain stitched with the night sky color patterns. Beyond it, the shadows of Tindinians bustled past.

A row of chairs faced the Mand lords' table, so the travelers quickly seated themselves.

"For love of Span," the Mands said in unison.

"And defense against Avid," Virallon returned. "My lords, thank you for meeting with us."

"It's rare indeed that we allow outsiders into our Great Hall," a gray-furred Mand replied in a growly voice. "But since the situation is dire and you have been sent by the Appon themselves, we welcome you. I am Lord Iwell. Have you been updated on the situation at the Time Tower?"

"No, we have not."

"Our scouts tell us that an army of Avid miscreants has gathered at the tower's base," Lord Iwell informed them. "They've been observed genuflecting to an individual that we suspect is the shapeshifter who first altered the clocks."

"Was he not destroyed?" Virallon asked.

"Apparently not."

"How do you know?"

"Because . . ." Here the Mand hesitated and looked at the others. "Because the alternative is impossible," he finished quietly.

"Because the creature resembles Lugis," a frail, white Mand explained. "He is the spitting image."

His words chilled Renna to the bone.

"By Alabass," Trujo muttered.

"Whom else could it be then, but a shapeshifter?" a grayish-gold Mand said. "Especially since ai lizard-like figure was spotted first, immediately after the sky dimmed. The lizard's description fits the Clock Keepers' original account."

"I see." Virallon's voice was grave.

It was daunting to learn that their enemy was so deranged as to shape himself after Lugis.

"Clock Keepers," Lord Iwell sneered. "The Appon should have allowed *us* to protect the clocks and none of this would have happened."

"Perhaps," Virallon said diplomatically. "But you do an admirable job defending the tower from here."

"How far is it across the moorlands to the tower?" Dunn asked after a moment.

"Only about a day's travel, which is why we have our soldiers stationed at the eastern wall alongside the Tindinian guards—despite our disagreements," Lord Iwell growled.

"But we shall send a squadron alongside you to the tower," his gray-gold companion declared. The rest of them nodded.

135

Renna's spirits rose a little at the thought of extra numbers.

"We gratefully accept this offer," Virallon said quickly.

"The mayor-council of Tindin have declined to send soldiers to assist you. They claim to need them all to defend the city from these persistent attacks," Lord Iwell said with contempt.

I'm sure they do, Renna thought as Virallon nodded.

The lords looked them over for a moment with their cat eyes and then studied each other.

"Were there not six of you summoned by the Appon?" the frail, white Mand asked. "Have you suffered a loss?"

The wound inside Renna throbbed as if he had jabbed at it.

Possibly my mother . . . and the man I loved.

"Lazzard Exlorid is missing," Trujo said.

"He departed from us in anger near the Ridge," Dunn added. "We do not know where he is now."

"My lords, we have reason to fear that this shapeshifter knows we are coming," Virallon said abruptly. "We discovered that the Krimmer was secretly a descendant of Lugis, and he became hostile when confronted."

The Mands murmured among themselves, disturbed.

"You believe that he has betrayed you and gone to join him?"

"It is a strong possibility," the Scrall told them. "Surely he at least alerted the villain."

Renna glanced at her other companions,

136

none of whom looked convinced.

"Then we shall instruct our soldiers to destroy him on sight," Lord Iwell declared, and the others grunted in agreement.

Renna gasped, just as Trujo bellowed, "What?"

Even Virallon grimaced at this hasty sentence.

"No," Sallindar said flatly. "We have no evidence that he's betrayed us."

The Mand lords regarded him coolly for a moment. Renna had a feeling they were unaccustomed to being told no.

"That is a risk we will not take," Lord Iwell told him, his feline gaze severe.

Biting her lip, Renna looked at Sallindar. His brow was dark and his jaw clenched, but he said nothing more.

"He won't return, Trujo," Virallon said. "Mark my words." He sounded less certain than his words, however.

"Dunn has the sight, not you," Trujo muttered in disgust.

Before Dunn could speak, a distant scream caught their ears. Renna gripped her staff, staring out the window.

"As you can see, we're constantly under attack," the gray-gold Mand said. He reached across the table and rang a handbell that rested in a cup.

"Our approval among the common Tindinians has risen of late," the white Mand said thoughtfully. "Only now do they understand our commitment to Span, when the worst has happened."

Shouts and more commotion followed outside before a yellow-furred soldier rushed into the meeting room. Her weapon—a long, three-pronged blade—was already drawn and ready.

"My lords, it's at the eastern wall," she said breathlessly. "Winged creatures!"

"How many?" Lord Iwell asked.

"Scores," she answered. "This is the largest assault we've seen. It's as if they're being fired from a cannon!"

"We will come to your aid," Virallon said immediately.

Renna jumped to her feet with the others. It occurred to her then, with a sinking heart, that an escalated attack was suspicious. If Lazzard *had* warned the shapeshifter of their presence, then this could very well be the result.

In a few moments, they were riding up to the wall that separated the city from the Time Tower's open moorland. Galopine guards lined the top of it along with Mands and other soldiers.

Over their heads, a storm of black wings raged. Monsters that resembled giant bats were dashing at the guards over and over again. Their features were closer to humans than bats, but the skin was stretched tight and skeletal, and their eyes were bright white. Their wings were leathery and their long claws yellow.

A volley of arrows repelled them briefly, but they attacked again seconds later.

"Della Von!" Virallon shouted, even as Renna recognized them from a drawing in a book.

Crowds of the cityfolk had gathered at a distance, watching in horror. The Della Von made

138

no screeching sounds; they were deadly silent, except for the wild and heavy flapping of wings. Their quiet focus made Renna's skin crawl.

From his horse, Dunn shot an arrow over the guards and into the midst of the bony wings. Sallindar vaulted from his saddle and began to scale the wall without the aid of the scattered ladders and ropes.

Renna shifted into her Umbra state as Trujo and Virallon took to the ladders. Then she joined them, climbing as fast as she could. Trujo struggled with his false leg, rung by rung, cursing.

"Where in Span is that Krimmer?" he demanded, dragging himself atop the city wall. The guards were startled by his bulk when he appeared beside them. He planted his mismatched feet and swung his axe through the neck of a diving Della Von.

Beside him, Renna spun her staff like a vortex. The beasts flew at her with claws out and pinions pummeling—she smashed wing bones and shoved her staff's end hard into stomachs.

A guard shouted nearby and stumbled off the wall. Then another was snatched up by yellow claws and Renna heard a terrible crunch. She didn't watch as the limp body fell.

Through the flashing of dark limbs, she suddenly caught sight of the Time Tower. It was a sinister spire in the distance, its gray stones framed by the unnatural twilight sky.

They were so close now. Her pulse quickened in encouragement, despite the continuing onslaught.

White fire blasted from Virallon, blinding

the Della Von even if he missed them. Stunned, they smacked into each other and fell, intertwined.

Then one Della Von suddenly broke through the line. It flew into the city, triumphantly spinning in the air.

The Tindinians cried out and fled as the beast flapped toward them. Dunn whirled and shot an arrow, then another, spearing it in the back. It dropped to the ground, just as one of its brethren plucked a Galopine guard from the wall.

Through her flashing staff, Renna saw Sallindar leap onto that creature's back. They wrestled for several seconds before the Della Von shrugged him off. He fell for one heartstopping instant—then he caught hold of a ledge.

Distracted, Renna parried a second too late. Fiery claws sliced through her side. She gasped, clapping her hand against the deep cuts.

Sallindar climbed back up onto the wall, one hand against his side as well. He was staring at her. She only had a second to notice before another winged brute flew at her.

Her ribs burned and stung as she fought, slowing her down.

What do we do if they don't stop coming? she thought desperately. *There's no magic meadow to put them to sleep!*

"Time for a shield, Virallon!" Trujo called out.

The Scrall cursed in reply as one of the creatures nearly grabbed him.

At that moment, the deep chime from a nearby clock reached the wall. Two Della Von flinched dramatically at the sound. It rang out again and one of them cowered for a moment, distracted. Trujo beheaded it with his axe just as light dawned on Renna: The Della Von didn't like the noise. Perhaps they hated any loud noise.

She whistled shrilly at the next one that attacked—it recoiled in the air, and she knocked it down easily with her staff.

"They don't like noise!" she shouted. "Make some noise!"

Trujo didn't need to be told twice—he roared at once and the guards joined in quickly. The Della Von hesitated, twisting and ducking their heads. They struck each other with their wings, confused, and fell victim to more blows.

Sallindar growled and Renna screamed, flinching at the pain in her side. The Della Von slashed at them aimlessly, clearly unable to focus.

At that moment, Virallon shouted a string of syllables. Then a massive explosion struck the air.

Renna ducked, nearly pitching forward off the wall. The barrage shook the stone beneath her boots for a moment.

But no debris came flying afterward. Her ears ached even as the roar tapered off.

She looked up, blinking in the searing silence. Where was the explosion? *What* was it?

The Della Von had disappeared. All the guards and her companions were huddled down low, except for Virallon. He just stood there, looking relieved.

Then he spoke into the ringing silence, and Renna had to strain to hear him: ". . . Just a noise spell. An amateur's trick." He lifted his chin defensively. "I have to conserve my strength for shield-casting."

Everyone stared at him for a moment, deafened and not quite understanding.

Then Trujo shouted, "Well done!" and a few others cheered.

Renna stood up painfully and gazed out toward the Time Tower, expecting to see a flock of the Della Von fleeing. But the sky was clear, except for a strange, pulsing bright line about thirty feet from the wall.

She looked down and saw a mass of the winged monsters lying on the ground below, unmoving. Virallon's trick had been powerful enough to kill them.

"Look!" Dunn said, pointing at the glowing streak in the air.

"What in Span is that?" Trujo asked.

"That's how they come through from Avid," a Galopine replied. "It's a crack in the border."

"We've seen a few others like that," a Mand added. "They split right open after the sky went dark."

Renna and her companions stared at the vertical slit hovering there, its brightness ebbing and increasing. The air around it wavered delicately, dangerously. Despite all the Avidian creatures they'd encountered so far, it was the first time a rift between the worlds had been visible.

She recalled now that the Rungers in the meadow had attacked in a similarly endless stream. Perhaps there had been a rift hidden in the tall grasses behind them.

"Can't we block it with something?" Trujo asked, scowling.

Virallon shook his head. "Resetting the clocks will seal them all. That is the only way."

"In the meantime, we guard it," a Mand growled. The other guards nodded, although they were clearly exhausted.

Beyond the fissure, the view of the moor was wide and clear, striking and sublime from atop the city wall. Stretching out for miles, the short, dark grasses waved uniformly in the breeze. Everything was flat and treeless, structureless, except for the tower. Since the lands around the Time Tower were forbidden to inhabit, distance served as an extra line of protection.

The tower stood like a stone blade struck into the ground. The shapeshifter's encampment at its base represented the hilt for that blade. Despite the distance, its inhabitants were visible stirring— some on the ground, some in the air—clustering in groups and breaking apart again.

The movement had the same rhythm as the pulsing of the crack between Span and Avid.

Renna took a shaky breath, staring out at the tower. A throb of pain reminded her of the fierce wound in her side; it was bleeding badly. It was time to be patched up before they set out across the moor.

Chapter Eleven

The hellions of Avid watched as Lugis climbed atop the back of a large Spinner. His movements were much more awkward than his appearance suggested, but he adopted a regal manner and clasped his blue hands together, gazing out at the stirring, restless mass. They snarled and jostled in their ranks, frequently falling into skirmishes.

The demons understood that Lugis was responsible for their strange, new freedom. There was strong magic in his unfamiliar scent: He reeked of sorcery and power in a way that drew them to him. He had opened up this brand new world to them, and it was ripe for the picking, filled with weaker beings that feared them.

Still the last of the delicious night air was calling. They longed to race out across the moorland in every direction—wild and mad and murderous.

"Let me feast on this beautiful sight!" Lugis crowed. "Look at you all, lined up like soldiers! Assembled at the foot of your commander's palace!"

145

Screeches and howls filled the air. Ghastly eyes caught fire and claws flashed in the darkness.

Sheer glee transformed Lugis's face into the toothy grin of Skink, delighting in his role. It was true: The Time Tower was now his palace, from which he could sit and rule over the chaos.

Soon there would be no councils, no laws, no *Appon . . . !* Soon all those who despised him and his kind would be gone.

The dark wonder of it swelled inside his chest. To his surprise, he levitated a few inches. He had forgotten that he could do that.

"Turn and face the great wide world I have given you," he commanded.

The mob rotated in a ramshackle, ungainly fashion, flapping, crawling, and sliding. As Skink gazed out over their multitude of heads, he suddenly stiffened.

There was movement out there in the thinning darkness. He could just distinguish a line of figures between the distant glow of Tindin and the horde gathered before him.

Who dared to stand between his army and their spoils? Tindinian soldiers? He would crush them like insects.

Ghoulish war cries exploded into the air, reminding him that the Avidians with night vision could see the figures much more clearly. The din deafened Skink until he crouched, covering his ears, and several Della Von collapsed to the ground.

*   *   *

Renna's blood curdled at the nightmarish

howls. Stalwart snorted nervously and the other horses veered inward toward each other. Yet the elderline leaves bandaged against the gash in her side sent an unexpected wave of calm through her.

She could barely make out her companions' grim faces or those of the twenty Mands that had joined them and led them through the gate in the Tindin wall. The tall, furred soldiers frequently murmured to each other and touched the symbols on their breast plates.

The company had ridden through most of the night, eating a hearty vegetable bread and drinking hot tea from their pouches, both of which the Mands had provided. Virallon had also drunk a strengthening elixir, to help him maintain any spells he cast. There had been no time to prepare further.

And they were still without Lazzard.

When Sallindar had tied the elderline dressing around her, Renna felt both the soothing force of the plant and the thrilling warmth of his closeness. She was embarrassed by the latter, but she stopped him a moment anyway to examine his own side. She remembered him clutching his ribs right after she'd been wounded.

He allowed her to lift his shirt, and her pulse quickened. But she found only the Swirl water pouch there, secured by a strap against his smooth, pale skin.

"You're not injured?" she asked.

He shook his head, not meeting her eyes.

She knew that this was significant, the fact that he had grabbed his side the same time that she had been slashed. What he had said in the Aggard Forest, that his kind could share sensations with those they loved . . .

It was a possibility too wondrous and incredible to fathom right now.

They were going into battle. She had no time to dwell on her rapidly swelling feelings for the quiet Tillen. Even though it was more than the attraction that flared up when he was close: It was his steadfastness and courage, the kindness revealed in his actions more than in words.

Nothing mattered now though but what lay directly ahead, and the fact that neither of them might survive.

She swallowed those emotions like hot stones, sliding into a semi-Umbra state in order to settle her mind.

A golden glow from the approaching morning colors fell upon the looming Time Tower and the mob beneath it. The latter was moving toward them.

Everyone drew their weapons.

The ground began to shake with the thunder of hoof and claw.

"By Alabass," Trujo muttered, reining in his shuddering mount.

The Scrall closed his eyes and began reciting his shield spell. He gestured and drew shapes in the air, focused on casting one much larger and stronger than any he had cast before. The others waited, breathless.

Sparks and flares appeared before them and then faded, the sky hues brightening overhead.

In their light, the fast-approaching horde took shape in a thousand unwelcome ways.

"I liked the look of that better in the dark!"

Trujo shouted.

"It's all the same to us," said a reddish-brown Mand named Kalip. With their cat eyes, the Mands' night vision surpassed even Sallindar's.

But now everyone could see the details: There were Spinners, Rungers, and more Della Von, as well as the giant grasshopper Jibbs. But that was all Renna recognized. Beyond that were disembodied, flying spikes; wheels of mismatched, violent limbs; huge, writhing snake and lizard beings; grunting man-sized worms; even some humanlike figures that were uniformly black, like living shadows . . .

Virallon's shield appeared like a bubble bursting in reverse, just as the monstrous army reached arrow range.

It was a magnificent dome of iridescence, but there was no time to admire it. Dunn and the Mand archers immediately fired arrows through its walls. Virallon continued to cast under his breath, urging his pony forward. Impressively, the shield moved with him, and its occupants followed at once.

The shield made contact with the creatures in a hollow smack, a satisfying portion of them falling backward into each other.

But the Scrall could not hold the protection for long, so its true purpose was to get close to the tower quickly. Renna leapt off Stalwart and rushed to the edge of the shimmering shelter. She swung her staff through it, crushing the nearest bones. Sallindar and Trujo did the same with their sword and axe, the Mands with their three-pronged blades.

The monsters up front stumbled backward

149

and fell, but others launched themselves at the shield from the back and sides. They wailed in frustration as they struck uselessly at the gleaming barrier.

Virallon pushed the shield further into the horde, as the champions and Mands fought through its front wall, pressing closer to the tower.

That structure overshadowed them now, with the sky hues reflecting off its own protective shield. The ancient magic cast over the stones hummed and vibrated softly above the one-sided battle.

"Virallon! Do not overextend yourself!" Dunn called out, nocking an arrow.

The Scrall still needed energy to defend himself, break through the shield on the tower, *and* fix the clocks. He made one last gesture and then dropped his gnarled hands.

"It's coming down!" Renna shouted in warning. She turned and whistled two short blasts at Stalwart, the signal to take cover. He raced away across the moor without further encouragement.

In an instant, the shield had collapsed around them. She took an instinctive step back.

The Avidian army hesitated for a moment, surprised. The Mands suddenly roared as they had upon the city wall and Trujo joined in, stamping his metal leg.

Then the monsters rushed at them in full force.

Fang, claw, horn, wing, coiled tail—Renna spiraled into the onslaught, her staff a punishing blur. Everything slashed her cloak, snagged her hair, tripped her. She ducked and rolled on the dew-damp ground, taking out many-legged beasts and breaking spindly legs.

She could not see the others, but she heard their voices above the outlandish cries. She heard blades sinking into bellies, Trujo cursing, Virallon shouting spells.

She took hits on all sides, pain burning in every limb. She sank deeper into her Umbra state, concentrating her focus away from the throbbing.

In the back of her mind, she wondered if Sallindar felt her own injuries in addition to hers. She pushed the thought aside as a nimble, indigo creature caught her eye, throwing its detachable claws. Astonished, she saw them slice through flesh and fly back to their owner.

Jibbs nearby were cracking ribs with a single kick of their armored legs. A furred behemoth with a row of four eyes rolled itself into a massive ball. Then it ploughed into one of the Mands.

She spotted Trujo—he was wobbling on his false leg but holding strong. He snatched up a Jibb and broke its back across his knee. The thing shrieked a horrible, chattering death-cry.

Renna reeled at the piercing sound and almost caught a blow in the face. A Della Von sank to the ground in agony.

More Jibbs attacked the Ralgir and he stumbled, tipping over. He roared defiantly, spinning his axe.

"I'll break all of your backs, even if I have to go deaf!"

At that moment, Renna stumbled into something unexpected: It was a rough canvas tent that flapped wildly in the wake of all the violent blows.

There were other makeshift shelters around it. They had reached the camp at the base of the tower.

A pale yellow Mand named Ilidia rushed forward between the tents, but a flying cylinder-shaped brute dived upon her. Sallindar launched himself with his sword slashing, bringing it down swiftly. Renna pushed in their direction, straining with the effort of holding off all sides at once.

A spider-like giant caught hold of her staff and yanked on it, but she kept her grip. She flipped the creature and smashed its head onto the ground.

Then a pair of strong legs kicked her in the stomach, knocking the wind out of her. She slammed the beast's face in, struggling to breathe as the next assailant struck. Wheezing, she forced herself to fight at the same speed. But she couldn't maintain it. She was gasping for air.

Arrows suddenly took out the beasts closest to her. She whirled as Dunn and the Mands rode past on their horses. Virallon was suddenly visible close by, fighting off a flying black spike the size of his head.

Breathless, she jumped and smashed it into pieces. Then she fell, blackness taking over her vision.

She desperately needed to catch her breath. But there was no time.

Something heavy sank its claws into her back. Agony shot through her and dropped her to her knees. She could not fight this demon on top of her, not without air. Fear engulfed her as she collapsed under its weight.

Then someone knocked the creature off. Sallindar was there and Trujo, yanking her to her feet. Suddenly, she could breathe again. The air rushed painfully back into her lungs. She staggered along with her companions, dizzy and frightened.

The pain in her back was astounding. She strained to regain her Umbra state and failed.

Trujo tripped over his metal leg and fell. She gasped at the effort to help him.

They were crashing through the rough shelters of the Avidians' camp. Virallon was shouting something. He was trying to cast a shield to give them a moment's rest, but the Mands were scattered, fighting—and dying.

Renna cried out as she caught sight of two of them lying prone under the battling creatures. There were horses too, and the fallen were being eaten.

She hoped desperately that Stalwart had gotten as far away as he could.

But the horde was thinning. Some of their ranks had taken off, heading for Tindin or anywhere else they could cause destruction without fighting so long and hard. A great many of them were also slain, the short grasses blotched with swaths of crimson and black.

The sky colors gleamed upon the sickening havoc below.

Dunn joined Renna, Sallindar, and Trujo; then about ten of the surviving Mands rushed up next to them. Virallon cast his shield as hastily as he could, his amber face wincing with the strain.

The shield bubbled up much smaller than

before, but it held. The Avidians smacked into it and collapsed backward.

More Mands came running, crying out wordlessly. Cursing, Virallon dropped the shield to allow them in; then he recast it immediately, wilting in his saddle.

Sallindar quickly crushed the monsters caught inside the new shield with them. The others collapsed, bloody and exhausted.

The Tillen sank to the ground himself a moment later.

Renna's clawed back burned and throbbed. Wincing, she got to her feet to look up at the tower. Its stone walls were not fifty feet away. They were so close now. They had to let Virallon begin to crack the tower's shield.

But how long would it take? Could they protect him in their battered states?

A sudden, booming voice cut through her thoughts.

"Well done! Well done!" the voice rang out into the air.

The mob attacking the shield slowed its efforts at once. All heads inside it turned quickly to see the speaker, but no one new had appeared.

"What a clever little force this is, outside my palace!" the voice exclaimed, delighted. "And look at those red badges. Of course. I should have known! The Appon gathered a *team!*"

This is the shapeshifter, Renna thought, trying to focus through the pain. She looked at her companions inside the wobbling shield. They were listening with their eyes glazed over.

"And is that a Scrall? How exciting. Such

worthy adversaries!" the voice continued.

His words took on a new meaning as Renna stared out over the sea of creatures. It dawned on her then that he was . . . surprised.

He had *not* been warned that they were coming.

"Show yourself, coward!" Trujo blurted, shaking his axe.

"Oh, I am quite visible! All you must do is you look up," the voice taunted.

Renna tilted her head to peer up at the Time Tower. Then she saw movement in one of the narrow windows.

The blue face of Lugis grinned eerily down at them.

A shiver raced through her. It was a shock to see that face in the flesh! Not in a drawing or a painting from the stories of old, not a description in an ancient song. There was the leering smile buried in the short beard and the black eyes bright against the blue skin.

She turned away in disgust.

"He did not know about us," Dunn said quietly, slumped on his horse.

Sallindar nodded, looking at Renna. "Lazzard did not betray us."

She smiled half-heartedly.

Trujo blinked, blood dripping from a great gash on his forehead.

"I knew it!" he bellowed.

At that, Virallon groaned and the shield suddenly vanished. Renna's heart sank as he slid off his mount and fell to the ground. Dunn reached him first and stood guard over him.

Renna drew again on her dwindling store of Umbra strength, backing up against Sallindar and Trujo.

They would not last much longer without the shield. Her heart pounded—her adrenaline spiked. It was the end of the line. But she would hold her ground as long as she could.

Then the shapeshifter called down from the window. "Hold!" he commanded.

To her surprise, the army obeyed. Some of the creatures lunged forward and stopped, frustrated. But most of them waited, drooling and gnashing their teeth. Whatever the reason for the delay, she was eternally grateful.

She took a deep breath and sank further into Umbra.

"See how well behaved my soldiers are? How loyal?" the voice crooned. "But they aren't *all* necessary for my defense, are they? I must allow them to go out into the world as promised."

He gestured dramatically out the window. "My Bitars will finish the job in a much more entertaining fashion."

On cue, three of the shadow-black, human-like figures emerged from the waiting mob. Renna realized she had not seen any of them fighting before. In fact, they appeared defenseless. They had no claws, teeth or weapons, only a black crest that fanned out behind their heads.

Like dancers, they each did a graceful spin, mesmerizingly cool and sinister.

"What in Span are those?" Kalip the Mand asked.

"Archaic fiends," Virallon gasped, scowling

at them.

"They only wish to dance with you!" the shapeshifter sang out.

The Bitars twirled again in sync as their brethren backed away reluctantly. Renna wondered if they hypnotized victims with their movements. She blinked hard, keeping her head clear.

"What do they do?" Trujo asked, holding his axe ready.

"They are some sort of parasite!" the Scrall called out.

A Bitar swept toward Dunn and Virallon, and the Heuwit swiftly shot an arrow. The Bitar wheeled aside, its reflexes like Sallindar's. Alarmingly fast, it danced up to Dunn's face and laughed despite having no mouth. It was a high, girlish laugh that echoed strangely.

The sound made Renna's skin crawl.

Then Dunn stiffened, his bright eyes wide. He was frozen in place.

The Bitar spun away from him, laughing again. As it moved, it suddenly transformed. In seconds, it had morphed into someone tall and muscled, with great, black antlers . . .

And its face bore Dunn's features!

An ebony, expressionless Dunn danced about in ecstatic movements, while the real Heuwit stood like a block of ice.

"Dunn!" Renna cried out. "What did it do to him?"

She lunged for the altered Bitar and struck it in the stomach with her staff. The creature doubled over, but the other Bitars burst into that same echoing laughter, pointing at Dunn.

Renna whirled to see the real Heuwit doubled over too, still frozen. She nearly dropped her staff in horror. Sallindar touched her arm, his bloody face grim.

"He will die if you kill the imposter," Virallon said wearily.

Dunn had been protecting him—now the Scrall moved protectively in front of the Heuwit, despite being dwarfed by him.

"Well, kill the others then!" Trujo yelled.

He and the Mands sprang forward and struck at the devilish dancers. But the Dunn imposter moved repeatedly into their way, slipping in between its companions and their weapons. They struggled not to strike it by mistake.

"Can we save him?" Renna asked Virallon, trying to straighten Dunn's stiff body.

"It must be temporary," he said, more to himself than to her. "It *must* be."

Her attempt to right the Heuwit shot pain through her in a thousand places. She gasped and Sallindar echoed it nearby. She stared at him . . . and this time, he met her eyes.

Longing, agony, and despair were locked together in that brown gaze.

The terrible laughter exploded again and then Trujo was frozen, his axe raised high. The nearest Bitar ballooned into the shape of a Ralgir and pivoted away from him.

A sob rose into Renna's throat. The Mands backed away quickly, afraid to keep fighting.

Sallindar growled, but Renna stopped him from lunging forward.

"They want us to attack them! We can't lose

158

you too," she said thickly.

He hesitated and gripped her hand with his four fingers, watching the Bitars dance.

The shapeshifter in the tower was laughing now, an irritating cackle that flew out over the moor. Renna glared up at the false Lugis in the window, hatred stirring her cloak all around her. She knew she needed to siphon that anger to keep herself from despair.

"You're a madman!" she screamed at him.

The shapeshifter guffawed even more, with a mania that belied his sculpted Lugis face.

"No, I am Skink!" he chortled. "I am Lugis! I am Skink! I am two in one!"

Then something caught Renna's eye. It swung through the air, flying around the back side of the tower.

She blinked and saw a familiar figure, sailing down toward them with his sword drawn.

In one fierce dive, he speared the last unchanged Bitar with his sword, straight through its black chest.

"Lazzard!" Virallon rasped in disbelief.

The other Bitars wailed in alarm as their companion hit the ground. Skink shouted furiously from the tower, but the dancers turned and bolted away through the other Avidians. All gracefulness disappeared as they fled, the two shadows of Dunn and Trujo.

"Cursed Krimmers!" Skink howled from his window. "Damn them to ashes!"

Lazzard hovered, staring up at him in surprise. He wore different clothes, and his green eyes were bagged and heavy, but he was whole.

159

Renna cheered up at him and he grinned wide, relief flooding his face.

"What's this? Happy to see me now?" he taunted.

Then a gray Mand named Maleri suddenly growled, surprising them.

"Traitor!" Maleri bellowed. "Spawn of Lugis!"

He threw a dagger, but Lazzard dodged and swooped away.

"Traitor!" the Mands all shouted, even as the other beasts rushed forward in the Bitars' wake. Thankfully, it distracted them from Lazzard.

"Get us to the tower door!" Virallon yelled up at him.

Renna braced herself for the new attack, desperately hoping she could hold her own.

Lazzard flew down and grabbed hold of first Virallon and then Sallindar, taking the latter by surprise.

"You can defend him best, Tillen!" he declared, flying off.

He was back in barely a moment and scooped up Renna, even as she fought. The ground dropped out from under her at a dizzying speed.

Clinging to his shoulders, her legs swinging, she called out to the fighting Mands, "Protect Dunn and Trujo! Protect them!"

Looking down, she saw horses and Trujo's Aloppin running after her and Lazzard, following from below.

"Dunn and Trujo," she gasped again as he set her down roughly.

"Yes, yes. Curse their heavy bones," he

160

muttered and flew back toward them.

The horses rushed in, snorting and screaming. Many had terrible wounds in their sides and haunches. Renna whistled two loud notes for Stalwart, the sound wobbling in her throat.

Then she joined Sallindar in guarding Virallon as he knelt at the tower's double doors. He was chanting forcefully, his yellow eyes shut tight.

The Avidians were no longer moving in unison; they were running wildly about the moorland, some attacking each other. But several continued the onslaught on the champions.

One of the claw-throwers descended upon Renna and Sallindar, whipping the air with its detached talons. The Tillen dodged them all, but Renna caught one in the thigh. She screamed and fell to one knee.

Virallon chanted louder, weaving his head back and forth.

Then Stalwart galloped into view just as Lazzard flew in low, bringing Trujo. The disruption caught the claw-thrower off guard, and Sallindar ran it through with his sword.

"Stalwart! Thank all the hearths of Toom!" Renna grabbed his reins and buried her face in his mane. Like the other mounts, he was slashed and bruised and trembling. But he was alive.

"What in Span happened to Trujo?" Lazzard shouted, dumping the frozen Ralgir. He had half carried, half dragged him on the ground. Without waiting for answer, he flew back for Dunn.

The syllables Virallon intoned were stranger and more twisted than any he had spoken before. The air was growing heavy around him.

The hairs on Renna's arms and the back of her neck shot upward and her cloak crackled strangely.

This was ancient magic, the kind that only the Scrall among them could wield.

The space between Virallon and the iron doors wavered as he rocked back and forth, chanting. His face was pale with fatigue and his hands shook.

"Look," Sallindar rasped, staring at Trujo. The Ralgir slowly blinked an eye and twitched a finger.

Renna grabbed his giant hand and squeezed it. Her small fingers could only grip one of his. Both their hands were bloody.

Lazzard dumped Dunn unceremoniously next to them and stood there exhausted. Moments later, five battered Mands rushed in. They turned on the Krimmer in a flash, three-pronged blades and bows drawn.

"Traitor!" they shouted.

"Stop!" Sallindar barked at them.

"Can't you see he's helping us?" Renna implored.

"We have our orders," an orange Mand growled. He flung his forked blade at Lazzard, but Sallindar leapt and knocked it out of the air.

"What is this? Who set these fur-bags against me?" Lazzard demanded.

"Spawn of Lugis!" Maleri accused him. "We know you deserted the mission!"

The Krimmer's face reddened. Then it blackened with fury. He lunged for Maleri with his sword, but Ilidia blocked him.

"Our lords directed us to kill you on sight!" she shouted. "You're lucky you—"

"Leave him alone!" Virallon suddenly roared, mid-chant.

Everyone jumped and stared at him. He ignored them and resumed the spell without missing a beat. Lazzard eyed him with a hopeful air, but he said nothing.

At that moment, a fanged worm the size of a pony reared at them, and the Mands busied themselves dispatching it.

"Where *were* you, Lazzard?" Renna asked him.

He shot her an indignant look. "I went where I was *welcome*, human! The taverns of Luder don't search their customers for signs of tainted blood!"

"Taverns!" she exclaimed, disgusted. "We needed you."

As she spoke, there came a rush of air like the release of a long-held sigh. The tower's thick coat of defense had finally dissolved.

Virallon lowered his head, drained, but there was grim satisfaction on his face.

Sallindar and Kalip shoved the tower doors open with a deafening iron groan. Renna pulled on Trujo's hand, with no real hope of getting him to his feet.

But he surprised her by squeezing hers back. Then his pointed ears wiggled.

"So, the Krimmer got drunk till he felt guilty enough to come back," he said thickly. "I should've guessed."

"Mind your tongue, oaf, or we'll leave you

outside," Lazzard snapped.

In a few moments, they had dragged themselves and the paralyzed Dunn into the tower, and the doors were slammed shut. Then everything was quiet.

There was a surreal stillness within the stone walls. No lanterns were lit, and only faint daylight drifted down from the windows above.

Directly before them was the entrance to a massive stone staircase that curved its way upward. On either side was a passage that presumably led to the Clock Keepers' sparse living chambers.

In the silence, Dunn slowly tilted his head, antlers scraping the stone wall. Renna heaved a sigh of relief.

They were all still here. Even the horses, except for Virallon's poor pony who was missing. The remaining animals huddled together in fear and the Aloppin had sunk to the floor in exhaustion.

"Patch yourselves up as quickly as you can," Virallon told them hoarsely. "We must reach the clock chamber at the top."

Chapter Twelve

There was a basin of water near each of the side passages and they took turns pouring stinging pouchfuls over their wounds. They stuffed the last of the elderline leaves into the group's remaining bandages and wrapped the more serious injuries.

Lazzard stood apart from the Mands, gripping his sword and watching them closely. They snarled at him but held off from further attack.

Moving gingerly, his eyes glazed, Sallindar bound a Mand's broken fingers and Dunn's twisted ankle. One of Virallon's eyes was swelled shut and his clothes were shredded and bloody. The deep rivets in Renna's back burned as if they were already festering, and the talon that had torn through her thigh gave her a severe limp.

There was no part of her body that did not hurt . . . and Sallindar carried that pain too.

She closed her eyes a moment and the darkness swam behind her eyelids.

When she opened them, Virallon was starting up the steps, his head held high despite his appearance.

But something came plummeting

downward: It was a fleshy mass of green and black, so large it almost filled the stairwell.

It was a *tentacle*—like that of a gigantic octopus.

The Scrall stumbled in shock and fell backward.

The sight of the impossible limb stopped Renna in her tracks. With suckers the size of her head, it lashed against the walls and lunged out at the group of them, hungrily.

The closest to Virallon, Trujo caught him up and pulled him out of reach.

"Is this some Avid abomination or the shapeshifter?" Lazzard demanded.

"This is *Skink*," Virallon growled, frustrated. He hurled a ball of sparks at the monstrous lobe, and it recoiled.

The Mands shouted as another tentacle tumbled down the stairs, striking the ceiling. Dunn and Maleri filled it with arrows. Lazzard flew forward and slashed through the thick flesh, spraying dark blood. Both tentacles writhed at the blows, but they did not shrink back.

"We must get past it!" Dunn shouted.

"Just tear it into ribbons," Trujo spat and sank his axe deep into a sucker.

Sallindar vaulted over the lower tentacle, but the upper one dropped to squeeze him between them. Renna rushed in and jabbed the top limb with her staff, slamming it into the wall.

"Bring Virallon!" Sallindar called to the others.

The slithering limbs closed in as the champions scrambled to get through them. Only a great deal of hacking could make them part briefly.

A third tentacle began its descent, but it was too large to get through. Renna pulled her knife from her boot and tried flaying the rubbery skin. Then the tentacle swung her hard against the wall.

Agony flared as her left arm broke against the hard stone. The pain shocked her out of Umbra. She was so bone-weary that it had already been slipping away from her.

"Curse this!" Lazzard shouted, spearing the tentacle over and over. "I can fly the Scrall up from the outside!"

As if in response, one of the tentacles shrank. It was a shuddering movement that knocked several of them off their footing. Now the width of a small tree, the lobe slapped itself around the Krimmer, holding him in place.

He barely had time to shout before the other tentacles did the same. One flew around Renna and pinned her arms, digging painfully into the fracture. The stairwell spun for a second and she nearly blacked out. She forced her focus to return as Dunn tried to cut her free.

Virallon let loose a string of fiery blasts, sending the third lobe coiling backward. Sallindar dragged him up the stairs in its wake. Over his shoulder the Scrall tossed two more, stunning the monstrous limbs enough to loosen their grips on Renna and Lazzard.

In another moment, they were all bolting up the steps, lashing backward at the tentacles that followed. Sallindar and Virallon lost ground and fell back into them; Trujo growled and pushed everything forward, tentacle flesh and companions alike. Renna was smothered and crushed repeatedly, struggling to stay on her feet.

Somehow the orange Mand was shoved backward and fell between the tentacles. They heard her armor crash painfully down the steps.

Then the tentacles shuddered and began to twist. They morphed rapidly into snakes. Pointed heads full of fangs popped up out of the coils. Renna cried out as one snapped at her—so fast it caught a chunk of her hair.

Virallon shrieked up ahead and Dunn groaned nearby, both bitten. Renna threw up her staff, one-handed, and braced it against the terrible reptile jaws. It took all her strength to hold them away from her.

Virallon was shouting something now. Renna's arm wobbled as the snake kept snapping at her. She couldn't hold out much longer. A cold sweat broke out all over her.

It was too much. They weren't going to make it.

The Scrall's voice was louder now, and the snake started to pulsate.

Then it vanished—so abruptly that Renna fell forward. She collapsed into Sallindar, who had just turned back to help her.

All of the snakes had disappeared.

She looked at him breathlessly. "What happened?"

He pointed behind him at a dark blue, lizard-like figure lying on the steps, panting. It bore terrible wounds all over its arms and legs, but somehow it got to its feet and raced away, up into the clock chamber.

Virallon had dispelled the shapeshifter's false forms, at the cost of even more of his strength.

"Is *that* the real demon?" Trujo shouted.

The group of them lurched after him, up the last of the steps. Then they found themselves in a large, round room with four columns and four arched windows.

Renna had expected understated grandeur, ancient and deteriorated. The only signs of that were the two elaborate woodworked screens on opposite sides. One depicted the Appon in crimson robes and the other, two spheres set apart from each other: Span and Avid.

Otherwise, the chamber was a disgusting mess, with a crude throne of bones, and refuge strewn everywhere.

Amid the chaos, the Two Great Clocks stood ticking quietly, framed on either side by a paralyzed Clock Keeper.

In every rendering Renna had seen of the clocks, they had been set one hour apart. It was shocking now to see their elegant hands in identical positions.

But there was no time to stare.

A ring of blue beasts that resembled dogs jumped to their feet near the throne of bones. They flooded the air with savage growls. Larger and more muscled than any dog Renna had seen, they bared multiple rows of teeth and lashed long, forked tails.

Behind them, Skink scrambled onto his makeshift throne. He was gangly and awkward, but his inky, reptilian face was keen, intelligent. He smiled gregariously, despite his injuries.

"Naturally, I'd prefer to appear as Lugis, but

this lowly shape shall have to do until that magic wears off," he declared. "Well done for now, Scrall. Show me what you can do to my Enja!"

"Save your strength," Dunn told Virallon quickly. Then he shot rapid-fire arrows into the pack.

The dogs halted briefly, absorbing the blows. Then they charged. With her unbroken arm, Renna swung her staff as best she could, while Sallindar and Trujo hacked wearily at the others.

They were fighting with much less vigor and speed, struggling to keep up with the demons.

With a sudden effort, Lazzard lifted Virallon and sailed over their heads toward the clocks.

"Curse all Krimmers!" Skink shouted and gestured at the Enja.

One of them sprang powerfully into the air, arrows protruding from its shoulders. It crashed into Lazzard and the Scrall just as they reached the clocks, sinking its teeth into Lazzard's leg. He screamed, the sound echoing against the stone walls.

Ilidia cried out too, as another Enja snapped his jaws on her wrist. It tore her hand off before she could stab its throat. Gasping, the Mand stared at her missing hand in horror.

As fast as she could, Renna caught up a corner of the Mand's cloak, stomped on one end, and tore it. She hastily wrapped the poor soldier's stump before another Enja could attack them both.

Sallindar vaulted over the backs of two Enja and drove his sword into the one that held Lazzard. The other two whipped around and lunged for him. Trujo felled one with an axe blow to the neck.

170

Virallon was chanting again. He reached up for the clocks with trembling hands. Once more, the air began to tremble with that strange, forgotten magic.

"Stop!" Skink exploded.

In a flash, he morphed into a Zin, blazing up from his throne. Then he hurled a ball of fire at the Scrall.

Virallon wailed, his hair and clothes ablaze. He began shouting the spell instead of chanting, his voice rasping in agony.

Sallindar tried to beat the flames from him, even as he held back the Enja gnashing its jaws in his face. Skink tossed another blazing ball—Virallon shrieked in misery.

Renna recoiled at the sound as she cracked the nearest Enja skull. It was the same made by Sallindar's horse, burning in Reegins Stone.

"Water!" Dunn cried. He fumbled with his drinking pouch as did the others. But all of them were empty.

The Scrall was still shouting the spell, shuddering as he burned. . . And an aura began to grow around the ticking timepieces.

The Enja loped away from the fire and smoke, frightened.

"Sallindar!" Renna shouted. "Use the Swirl!"

It was the only water anyone had left.

The Tillen tore the secret pouch from inside his shirt. Then he dumped it fully over Virallon, extinguishing the fire. The colored water splashed the clocks as well, gleaming with a staggering brightness.

Sallindar's pale skin brightened too—he was suddenly ghostly.

"What . . . is . . . *that?*" the Zin-Skink crackled.

Virallon gasped in pitiful relief. He was huddled in pain and spasming, but still he chanted. The radiance of the Swirl water intensified the aura around the clocks.

The Enja were cowering in a corner now, even though the fire was out. Skink screamed at them to attack, but they sensed that something had changed. The balance had shifted.

Renna slumped to her knees, her staff dragging on the ground.

"What's happening?" Lazzard asked, alarmed. His hands were clamped against his bleeding leg.

"The Swirl's enhancing his magic," Sallindar breathed.

Moving like someone in a dream, Virallon touched the hour hand of the Avid clock and began to shift it.

Skink launched himself at him, Zin flames shooting through the air.

Then the room tore apart at the center.

A swath of night sky streaked over their heads, just below the ceiling of the chamber. But it was not right, not Span's sky . . . There were no colors in the panel of darkness, no Great Kenda or any other pattern that Renna knew.

Instead, there were thousands of tiny, white lights embedded in the blackness. They were shrouded by violet storm clouds, swirling rapidly.

The sight dazzled her beyond any

172

comprehension. She could not make sense of it.

"Dunn . . . is this a vision?" Trujo asked.

The Heuwit shook his head slowly.

"It is *Avid!*" Virallon shouted, his voice cracking. "It's a massive rift!"

Lightning cracked across the storm clouds, splintering into a thousand forks. Through the rift, the ground was suddenly visible below. That ground was teeming with life, swarms of grotesque beings battling each other in the storm.

Every fiend that had fought in the moorland was visible, every demon that had appeared on the journey to the tower, and countless, unrecognizable others. They were tearing, stabbing, chasing, and crushing, reveling in the destruction and the chaos.

Avid was a world of war. Its beasts knew of nothing else.

The lightning illuminated them again and again. Then the rain deluged so violently that the fighting was suddenly asea, churning in bloody waves.

Renna shrank from the breach in horror. She couldn't breathe, her knees tucked up into her chest like a child. It was so dangerously close, so real, though it hovered in the air like an illusion.

Then Skink transformed back into Lugis, a battered and broken version. He gazed through the rift, enraptured, his wild eyes doubled in size.

"Oh, magnificent Avid!" he purred. "What delicious destruction! So pure! So perfect!"

One of the Enja howled suddenly. Then it darted across the room. Renna stared as it jumped and flew into the breach, disappearing into the stormy darkness.

Another one followed, and then another. Then the rest of the dogs rushed for the rift, all of them frothing at the mouth.

"Yes, let us go!" Skink cried out, ecstatic. He stepped away from the clocks and reached out toward the rift. "It is where I belong!"

At that moment, Virallon shoved the hour hand of Avid's clock as fast as he could.

All the way around.

The luminescence that enveloped both the clocks swelled instantly, irradiant and blinding. Renna shielded her eyes, and then buried her face into her knees.

Skink spun around with his jaw dropped.

The Clock Keepers snapped awake—then collapsed onto the floor.

The portal into Avid closed as swiftly as it had opened. In seconds, the great gash sealed itself and vanished.

Then the chamber was perfectly still. No nightmare vision hung over their heads.

The brilliant aura faded a heartbeat later. Then the clocks ticked quietly again—one hour apart.

A strangled scream burst from Skink. He raised an arm to strike Virallon, his face livid.

But Sallindar was faster. In the blink of an eye, he stabbed Skink through the heart.

The shapeshifter wobbled, astonished. Slowly, painfully, the features of Lugis collapsed inward on themselves. He was Skink again. After a few seconds, he fell backward onto the stone floor.

Renna gazed at him numbly for several long moments. He was completely still.

"Is it over?" Trujo asked in a low voice.

Trembling, with severe burns all over his face and arms, Virallon nodded his head. Sallindar was quiet, his own glow slowly fading from his skin.

"We did it," Lazzard breathed, incredulous. "We did it."

"For love of Span," the Mands murmured, low.

Renna sighed, too much in shock to celebrate.

"We must take you to a healer," Dunn told the Scrall in a daze. He himself was bleeding freely from a snake bite in the shoulder.

"Our lords will send help," Maleri murmured.

Next to him, Ilidia gasped, huddled over her stump of a hand. Renna turned toward her, and shakily tried to bind her wrist tighter. She couldn't move her own left arm without fierce pain.

"Are the . . . are the Clock Keepers alive?" she asked over her shoulder.

Sallindar prodded them both and they stirred but did not seem conscious.

A new movement suddenly caught Renna's eye.

It was Skink's body, morphing again.

"No!" she shouted, gripping her staff.

The others gasped and lifted their weapons.

How could he have survived such a blow? Was he *immortal?*

But the shapeshifter did not move again. In fact, he had simply shifted one last time—into a dark-haired . . . female . . . Krimmer.

175

"What in Span?" Trujo exclaimed.

The Krimmer lay flat on her back in the same position as Skink, eyes glazed over in death. She was naked except for the light feather down that Lazzard shared.

Renna could not believe her eyes.

Lazzard stared hard. He slid forward quickly to study the body. Then his face went deathly pale.

"How could he transform if he is dead?" Dunn asked, his arrow still notched and aimed.

"It's his true self," Sallindar said quietly. Then he glanced at Lazzard.

"*Her* true self," Renna said, amazed. She remembered now how she had questioned the assumption that Skink was male.

Lazzard screwed his eyes shut tight and hung his head.

"But the Scrall's spell on the stairs?" Maleri asked, bewildered. "Didn't that remove his false shapes?"

Virallon said nothing, unable to explain.

"I imagine . . . she hasn't worn this shape in many, many years," Lazzard said quietly. "This is my cousin. The one who went mad and disappeared when I was a child."

"Oh, no," Renna murmured.

"Your *cousin?*" Kalip echoed in disgust.

"Dalzina Exlorid."

Lazzard reached over and closed the dead Krimmer's eyes. They were blue instead of green, but just as bright as his.

"She was beaten by a mob for being a descendent of Lugis and it damaged her brain." His voice was flat, expressionless. "I would wager that she forgot she was once a Krimmer long ago."

Renna couldn't help but look at Virallon, whose scalded face was pinched with guilt and misery. The others glanced at each other helplessly.

Lazzard may not have betrayed them, but another of his lineage was guilty—because she'd been tortured by those that hated her lineage. Yet the news would be so much more damaging for those who bore the mark of their terrible ancestor.

Virallon struggled to his feet, holding on to Dunn's arm. His swollen eyes moved from Dalzina to Lazzard and then toward the nearest window. All their eyes followed and blinked in the restored brightness of the sky.

"We will tell no one of this," he croaked finally. "We will burn this body and speak only of a deranged shapeshifter with unusual gifts."

His voice was ravaged, but his words were as golden as the daylight that pooled into the room.

Chapter Thirteen

The morning sky colors awakened Renna two days later, in a large room at an inn. For a few seconds, it was luxurious and wonderful . . . Then every bone and muscle in her body whimpered in pain.

She was clean and bandaged, but her injuries would be slow to heal. Some she had not even been aware of: two broken fingers, a bruised rib, pulled muscles in her upper back and shoulders.

There was a splint on her left arm and the gashes in her back and her side had been stitched neatly by a Tindinian doctor. A strong sleep draught had done her a great deal of good, but now she wasn't sure she could even get up without aid.

Gingerly, she turned her head to see the other beds in the room. Trujo was snoring like a trumpet, but Virallon was not there to talk in his sleep. He had remained voluntarily in the Time Tower, along with the slowly awakening Clock Keepers and a new group of Tindinian soldiers. There he slept in a cot at the foot of the clocks, wearing a full-body suit of bandages. His severe burns had been slathered with many soothing lotions and herbs, but their benefits were limited.

It was very possible that magical treatments could prevent him from being permanently disfigured, but Renna imagined that he wasn't much concerned about that. She had developed an intense admiration for the fractious Scrall and his "perseverance in all matters."

Dunn wheezed softly in the bed next to Trujo, propped upright to protect his badly bitten shoulder. Lazzard was out cold with his wrapped leg resting on extra pillows.

But Sallindar sat up slowly in his blankets, blinking at her. Then he cringed as the movement dug into his own wounds. The black bruise on his jaw and the scratches on his forehead did not mar his fine-boned features in the slightest, to her eyes.

She smiled, her blood tingling with the incredible relief that they were alive . . . and with the thrill of their quiet eye contact in a peaceful room.

Soundlessly, he slid out of his bed and came to hers, wincing at each step. Her pulse quickened as he slid under the blankets beside her, his body warmth easing her soreness. They embraced as gently as two battered lovers could, Renna giggling at their pitiful state.

"I wake when you wake," he whispered in her ear.

"And you ache when I ache?" she murmured, pressing her face into his flushed neck.

"Yes."

That simple, sincere declaration—the antithesis of Callin's quick dismissal—was a balm that soothed most of her frayed edges. But not all.

"We can search for your mother together," he said, as if reading her thoughts.

She kissed him tentatively, uncertain whether Tillen did such a thing. He responded readily enough, and her heart danced.

Whatever happened now, this fiercely capable, gentle spirit was by her side. It was a gift she had never imagined possible. Certainly not from a revered race like the Tillen, who could very well consider humans beneath them.

She was worthy. She had done her part in saving Span and she had survived.

Perhaps the Appon had summoned its champions wisely after all.

With their foreheads pressed together, she pictured him in the clock chamber with his skin alight as the Swirl water splashed the clocks.

"Why did you glow when you used the Swirl water?" she asked him softly.

"I don't know," he said, frowning. "I could feel it . . . mingling with the clocks' magic, making it stronger. I also heard voices, but they spoke so quickly." His brows furrowed, trying to recall. "They said that Span was an inner realm, hidden from the . . . stars."

"Stars?" Renna asked, drifting into a half-sleep.

"And they called me Kin-of-Kin."

She barely heard the last words, dosing in his arms for a short while. She dreamed of the sunny meadow in the Aggard Forest, of soft grass and sparkling, winged creatures.

Sallindar shifted suddenly, and she awoke. He had turned to stare at Dunn, whose misty eyes were wide open. He was gazing ahead in that familiar fashion, spying on an invisible future.

"A vision?" Renna asked, her voice thick with sleep. "Don't tell me we have to fight again."

"The clocks . . . " Dunn said, tilting his antlers. "I see the two clocks . . . taken from the tower."

Renna's head dropped to her pillow, the lightness fading from her heart.

"Where are they?" Sallindar asked. He got to his feet unsteadily.

"In water," Dunn replied wonderingly. "They are standing in . . . Swirl waters."

Renna caught her breath and raised her head, meeting Sallindar's eyes.

"They are in the Swirl," Dunn said with a slight smile. "And they are safe."

*   *   *

The champions rejoined the Scrall in the Time Tower a week later, accompanied by the Mand lords and the mayor-council of Tindin. The sky was brilliant and clear in a glorious dome overhead, as if even the elements of Span—not just its inhabitants—were celebrating their separation once again from the terror of Avid.

The dark gray tower was no longer sinister under a diluted sky. Now it embodied the reassuring fortress that Renna had always imagined, and it welcomed them like a beacon as they rode in ceremony over the moor.

The Appon were expected to join them in the clock chamber by astral projection, to discuss

Dunn's vision and the future of the clocks.

The Tindinian's mayor-council consisted of three Galopines, two Klydeers, and one human, all wearing brown cloaks with green pins at their collars. They rode together in one large open carriage and the Mand lords rode in another, both accompanied by soldiers on horseback.

Ilidia was one of those soldiers and she waved her remaining hand at Renna. Renna waved back, happy to see her yellow fur clean of blood and shining.

Of the three Mands in the clock chamber battle, she had been the first to accept Virallon's demand for secrecy about Dalzina Exlorid— possibly out of gratitude for Renna's aid.

Renna and her companions rode in a third carriage, their own steeds resting in a Tindinian stable. She leaned against Sallindar a moment, ignoring the pain the movement caused. Everyone was as cleaned up as could possibly be, but it only made their injuries that much more noticeable.

Trujo had also received a brand new false leg, made of a stronger alloy. It was shaped into a rough foot at the end, and he was rather pleased with it.

When they reached the tower and climbed out of the carriage, the Ralgir grinned smugly at Renna, revealing missing teeth. She realized then that she was holding Sallindar's hand. She blushed at this first public sign of their attachment.

Trujo elbowed Lazzard and nodded his head at them.

"What's this?" Lazzard raised an eyebrow.

Sallindar ignored them as they passed

through the doors.

This time, the tower was well-lit by sconces on the walls. That alone made a remarkable contrast, but the staircase that had seemed so insurmountable before was also wide open and clean. There were no blood stains or snake scales or signs of struggle . . .

Renna blinked at the polished steps, trying to clear the nightmare of it all from her mind.

"I thought I was informed of everything I missed, Trujo," Lazzard was saying. He smirked at Renna, pulling her out of her thoughts.

"I was there the whole time, but this is new," Trujo said, amused. "I bet Dunn saw it coming."

The Heuwit smiled and Renna realized, to her surprise, that it was the first time she had seen him do so. It was a little unsettling; like certain types of deer, he had no teeth in his upper jaw, but a palette made for grinding plants.

"No. Never have I had a vision of a Tillen and human union," he said.

"It makes sense. They're both tiny," Trujo declared.

"You're talking about me as if I wasn't here again," Renna told them, but she couldn't help smiling. She knew that her face was bright red.

"So tell me, Sallindar, if I were to strike Renna down, then would you feel it?" Lazzard asked as they reached the clock chamber.

"You'd be lucky to get as far as the first part," Sallindar said with a fierce grin. Renna laughed and squeezed his hand.

Lazzard rolled his eyes. "Perhaps the two of

you should consider a more peaceful lifestyle."

He was hushed then by others crowding into the round chamber with them. Renna found herself staring up at the domed ceiling where the terrifying rift into Avid had opened.

She heard the lightning crack and the screams of the thousand warring beasts . . . then she dropped her gaze.

The Clock Keeper Anderin stood beside the imposing timepieces, which ticked quietly. Virallon sat in a padded chair nearby, wrapped in gauze. Renna expected him to look more severe than ever, considering the pain he was in. Yet the deepest furrows in his face seemed smoother now and softened. He appeared to be more at peace than Renna had ever seen.

Trujo waved at him over the rows of heads in the chamber, and Virallon nodded back, unbothered by the lack of decorum.

Before them, a dais waited expectantly. The silence in the chamber deepened and Renna realized she was holding her breath.

Several long moments passed before a soft ball of light appeared above the dais, hovering in the air. It glowed white at first, but gradually it became red. Then it deepened into the crimson of the Appon badges that Renna and the others still wore.

Slowly it expanded until it formed a cloud large enough to block the dais from view. Several Appon faces appeared within it and wavered solemnly, their calm, white eyes a welcome sight.

The small crowd murmured in admiration. The vapor around the Appon gently faded until only their faces remained, awash in that warm red light.

"Greetings to you all," the Appon with the deep, rich tone spoke.

His voice was an unexpected, dizzying reminder of that day at the Observatory Hearth. Renna recalled how terrified she had been to hear them call her name—how out of place and inferior she had felt.

Everything was different now.

"It is with great relief and joy that we greet you in this most precious of chambers!" the Appon declared. "For we are alive in the time of a new legend, one that will be passed on to our children and our children's children."

Goosebumps raced up Renna's arms. *A new legend.*

"As Santir once defeated Lugis," he continued. "So have our champions rescued the clocks from his dark disciple's clutches!"

A great cheer roared through the chamber. Renna's cheeks burned red for the second time that morning. She laughed, flustered and overwhelmed.

Hands clapped, boots stomped, whistles blew, and all faces turned to smile at her and the other champions. She smiled back and nodded, leaning against Sallindar. He put one arm around her and touched his necklace pendant with his other hand.

"Envoys and other messengers have been sent far and wide to spread this wonderful news!" the Appon added.

Trujo stamped his false leg along with the crowd's continued acclamation.

"Make sure they hear it in Alabass!" he

called out, and clapped Lazzard on the back.

The Krimmer threw up his arms in mock protest at the applause. Then he bowed extravagantly.

But Renna noticed that his eyes were sad. She thought of his cousin's body burning to ashes on the stone floor, so close to where the dais stood now. Lazzard had said his goodbye and Dunn had set the dead Krimmer aflame. Then they had buried the ashes without a trace behind the tower.

It was Virallon's unspoken apology to Lazzard for his prejudice. They would keep the secret forever and spare his unfortunate bloodline from greater harm.

"As you are aware, we cannot maintain our presence in this form for long," a different member of the Appon spoke. "Therefore, we must discuss the new plan regarding the protection of the clocks."

The cheering died down and the room gradually turned quiet again.

"Our esteemed Clock Keepers have proven not to be infallible after all. Too great a spark of life manifested inside the one called Elix, and he became unsatisfied with a life that existed solely for one purpose. This was unforeseen and a grave mistake on our part. He is being transported to the Observatory Hearth for us to examine."

Anderin, so expressionless and still, suddenly lowered his head. Whether it was in grief or shame, no one could tell. He was only vaguely aware himself. His mind was a soft swirl of melodies, colors, and numbers.

"And now we must address the unexpected

event that occurred in this chamber when the waters of a Swirl splashed upon the clocks," the sweet-toned Appon declared. "As you may or may not know, Swirls do not exist in the dark realm of Avid, where the only light comes from distant stars."

There was that word again, *stars*. Perhaps they were the white lights in the sky that Renna had glimpsed through the rift.

"But here in Span, the Swirls have long been known as the source of our sky hues, as well as the colors in all our flora and fauna. And we have often suspected that they are the source of life itself in Span, and most closely connected to its original creatures."

Surprised murmurs began to spread throughout the chamber. Renna glanced at Sallindar who had tensed beside her.

"Not long after we first arrived in Span, we began to study the murmuring voices of the Swirls," the Appon continued. "Eventually we came to the conclusion that they belong to the souls of the unknown beings that first created this realm, perhaps for the same kind of refuge that we needed. We believe these souls may impart knowledge and wisdom when it's most needed, but only to those who can understand them. Perhaps those most closely connected to Span itself."

Renna squeezed Sallindar's hand, and he clenched hers back.

"When Sallindar the Tillen poured the water from a Swirl onto Virallon Maggan and the clocks, those spirits gave us an apparent warning," a different Appon spoke up. "They tore open a hole wide enough for all those present to witness the terror of Avid, to remind them of the dangers of exposing Span."

As the assembly absorbed this, the heads of the Appon turned slowly to look at Dunn. He nodded respectfully.

"Dunn the Heuwit, with his prophetic vision, has shown us what is perhaps a better way to keep our realm safe from its sister world," the Appon announced. "The largest known Swirl is located near his homeland, Mustin. In accordance with his vision, the Mands shall transport the clocks to this special wellspring and place them directly in its waters. Lord Iwell has informed us that his kind will make a new home there and watch over the clocks all their days."

Someone prodded Renna's elbow as she listened, and she turned to see a Galopine messenger beside her. He handed her a letter, nodded with his long feelers, and then squeezed back through the crowd.

Renna stared down at the folded paper as the rest of the assembly cheered again. Fingers trembling, she tore it open.

"For the Appon champion of Umbra Combat, Renna Estarlin. The survivors of the human village Toom have been housed in Accrim. Nothing is known of the Umbra trainer or Callin Ider specifically, but all those trained in combat are said to have departed to join the fight against Avidian invaders.

One individual remains in Accrim with the name Estarlin."

The clock chamber reeled around Renna as she read the words. She read them three times over to be sure.

Then she turned to Sallindar, her eyes bright as the waters of a Swirl.

"She's alive!" she whispered.

No further announcements from the Appon mattered to her now.

"Sallinder, my mother is alive!"

###

Acknowledgements

I am forever grateful to my incredible support system: my true love Robert, my amazing family, my best friends, and my band members, all of whom have continued to root for me despite my many blunders. I don't know how I got so lucky. I also want to thank anyone who has enjoyed my books and shared them with others. Thank you for appreciating these little worlds and for helping them grow.

About The Author

Simone Snaith is an author of Fantasy, Urban Fantasy, and Young Adult novels. She lives in Los Angeles with her fiancé, a ridiculous amount of CDs and books, and two squabbling tuxedo cats. She also sings in the pop/rock band Turning Violet.

More info on the cover artist, Audrey Knight, is available at audreyknight.com.